T0117132

ECONOMICS AS A SECOND LANGUAGE

WRITTEN BY

Anderson Hitchcock

"Building Wealth, One Family Reunion at a time"

iUniverse, Inc.
New York   Bloomington

Economics as a Second Language (ESL)

iUniverse books may be ordered through booksellers or by contacting:

iUniverse
1663 Liberty Drive
Bloomington, IN 47403
www.iuniverse.com
1-800-Authors (1-800-288-4677)

ISBN: 978-1-4401-9188-6 (sc)
ISBN: 978-1-4401-9189-3 (ebook)

Printed in the United States of America

iUniverse rev. date: 12/28/09

IN MEMORY

I'll never forget my parents saying to me on more than one occasion, "Boy what do you think, money grows on trees? Little did I know then the significance this saying would have on my life? It has become the reason for much that I do on a day to day basis. Within this saying is the kernel for the idea, the acorn for the mighty oak, I continue to develop through the Institute for Economics as a Second Language, Inc., namely Family Corporations. Money indeed does grow on trees – Family Trees. Shake your family tree today and see what falls out.

This book is written in memory of Mrs. Lula Mae Hitchcock, my mother, who throughout her life taught me the value of never losing sight of ones dreams. She encouraged me, both in words and in deeds, to continue to pursue this book and this subject matter. She sat patiently as I bounced ideas off of her on the front porch of her home in Chagrin Falls, Ohio.

Mother I love you for your kind caring nature, and for the spirit of perseverance and pure grit that you instilled in me and in all of your children, both those you bore biologically and those who claimed you as their mother after being birthed by others. You were indeed a universal mother, who cared deeply about the pain and suffering of individuals, regardless of what race, creed or color they happened to be.

Felton Hitchcock Sr., my father, deserves credit for raising me with a stern upbringing which helped me to see the value in hard work, for as a plumber, electrician and mechanic he helped me at an early age to realize that I wanted to find my calling in a profession other than as a manual laborer.

As a result of that upbringing I have attempted, sometimes successfully, to live in the world of ideas, where everything becomes possible and nothing is ever out of reach. If you are reading this book, I encourage you to pursue your dreams and never stop trying to make the world a better place in which to live.

DEDICATION

This book is dedicated to Daniel Berry, former associate director at the George Gund foundation in Cleveland, Ohio. Mr. Berry recognized the potential in me and in the concept of ESL at the early stages of my development and the development of ESL.

During my graduate work at Case Western Reserve University, Mandel Center for Non Profit Management, Mr. Berry, became my mentor and thought so much of my ability as a theorist and practitioner of economic theory that he brought me into the foundation as an intern program officer in community economic development. This year long experience contributed greatly to my appreciation for the work of foundations in developing social policy and economic networks in order to alleviate some of the inadequacies of an economic system whose major motivation is profit.

Through Mr. Berry I received my first grant from a foundation. The initial grant allowed me to develop the Family Reunion Use Survey and to travel to Black Family Reunion Festivals, being sponsored by the National Council of Negro Women in cities throughout the United States. The data gathered is represented in the first comprehensive report on the spending power connected with the Family Reunion Movement in American written in 1996, with the aid and assistance of Princess Jones, a public policy analyses in the Washington, D.C. area.

Juan Barrientes and Dora Castro helped me to shape my earliest thoughts about community economic empowerment during the space of nearly two years, while I worked for them at Casa Rasa, a community service organization in San Jose, California. Juan and Dora accepted me as a full member of their staff and exposed me to the wonderful and caring culture of the Hispanic community of San Jose.

It was during some late night discussions around the dinner table that the concept of ESL as an economic tool began to be formed. It was quickly realized that regardless of what ones primary language happens to be, it is necessary to be conversant in the language and concepts of how real wealth in formed. As it was termed by one staff member, named Ralph, "the ditters and the gitters" determine our ability to fulfill our mission as an organization, or as an individual. Thus began the nearly twenty year odyssey that brings us to the writing of this book.

John Threadgill, stimulated my initial interest in how a family corporation might work, when as an advisor to an organization named ECHO, Inc., the Economic Community Humanitarian Organization, upon whose board of directors I sat in the early 1980's, he expounded at length about how his family had purchased a house in San Francisco as a fixer upper, and after all the family members had pitched in to paint and remodel the property, they decided to place the house in a family trust. They now own numerous other properties through their family trust, which is now worth several million dollars.

I must acknowledge the leading role that has been played by Dr. Ione Vargas, Professor Emeritus at Temple University, in the popularizing of the concept of the family reunion. For nearly twenty years Dr. Vargas has lead an effort of research and coordination of the sociological impact of family reunions in the African American community. Without her excellent leadership in this field, I am sure that the research on the family reunion phenomenon would not have gotten to the point at which we now find it. To Dr. Vargas is owed a debt of gratitude by all those who now benefit from her early research, including myself.

Pastor Joan Salmon Campbell, a Presbyterian Minister, provided office space and support for the Institute for Economics as a Second Language, Inc. as it got off the ground in Cleveland, Ohio in 1995. Without her support I am not sure that we would have ever gotten to the point at which we now find ourselves.

The prayers of the righteous availeth much, so says a passage in the bible. Well if that is the case, and I believe that it is, Ms. Elsie Dixon Bowen must be given credit not only for her prayerful efforts on behalf of me and the concept, but also because of her untiring financial support. On a salary derived from her in home day care business, Ms. Dixon never failed, as a member of the advisory Board of the Institute, to assist with the bills of the organization.

Emart Harley, of the Harley Corporation and an advisor to IESL, Inc. must be singled out for his support and for his friendship. Mr. Harley always believed in me and in what I was trying to do and encouraged me to continue moving forward, and for that I am eternally grateful.

Cynthia Gilhool, whom I met during a brief stint at the March of Dimes, played an invaluable role as a consultant and advisor to IESL. Ms. Gilhool spent countless hours with me massaging this concept, writing proposal, grants, work plans and more, that helped to shape my thinking and the future of this organization. I gratefully acknowledge that without her assistance success was anything but guaranteed.

Angela Darling, of the Bronx in New York, has played and continues to play an important role in spreading the message of IESL. Angela has formed a New York Chapter of the Institute and in addition to her primary function as founder and director of Love Your Breasts, Inc. a not for profit organization dedicated to spreading the word about breast cancer in minority communities throughout the United States, Ms Darling has been a tireless advocate of ESL.

Lastly, I want to send out a special dedication to the person who has been most responsible for insisting, cajoling, arm-twisting, supporting and believing in me and the need for the work that I am doing, and that is Ms. Etha Robinson.

Ms. Robinson is a teacher at Dorsey high school in Los Angeles, and is the founder and director of the African American Food Association. Etha is one of the great unsung heroes of the struggle to coalesce African Americans into a force for political, economic and social change.

Far more than any other individual that I can name, Ms. Etha Robinson deserves a debt of gratitude from me and from all those who wish to see family reunions take on a greater role in the quest for economic, social and spiritual renewal in our communities. She has been on the front lines of the fight to save our young people from crime, drugs, unwanted pregnancies and inattentive parents for over thirty years.

She has still found the time, the energy and the financial where with all, to provide IESL with a true patron saint. I have found her to be compassionate to a fault, trust worthy beyond belief and committed 110% to the cause of our race. Let no one ever doubt the importance attached to the support given to IESL, by its strongest support, Ms. Etha Robinson.

Wilma Ardine Kirchhoffer and Guy Marbury, of Youth Leadership for Global Health, Inc. of Atlanta, Georgia must be recognized for the support that they have given to IESL. Ms. Kirchhoffer, in agreeing to write the forward for ESL demonstrates an unwavering support for the family reunion concept. Mr. Marbury has through his words and actions played an indispensable role in ESL.

I want to express my heart felt thanks to Wilma Ardine for her kind consent to write the forward for this book. Youth Leadership for Global Health, Inc. of which she is the co-founder and Executive Director, is an organization very much in keeping with the goals and objectives for which IESL was established, and to that end we support all of the marvelous work that they are doing with that not for profit organization.

CONTENTS

FORWARD

Wilma Ardine Kirchhofer, MPH, Ph.D

When Anderson Hitchcock first extolled the basis for Economics as a Second Language, I could only think – finally, an answer to an age-old obstacle to the generation of wealth in our community! Most of my life, I have heard the statistics on the flow of money out of our communities. I've heard the laments about not leaving a financial foundation for our children to build upon. Being the daughter of owners of a small restaurant, I immediately understood why Anderson was so excited. I could actually feel this zeal through the telephone. Even though I had not yet met Anderson face to face, I could see the light shining in the sounds of his words. I could feel a blessing on the make for our community.

Our communities cannot apply economics when the principles of economics are ignored or misunderstood! We must study economics just like we are learning a new language-the language of income and wealth generation. Anderson clearly explains the timeless methods to make money your servant – a servant that benefits your family and your community.

Shortly after the telephone conversation, we were able to spend a day with Anderson in Chester, Pennsylvania. It was there he outlined the dynamics of converting the spending power inherent in family reunions into family corporations that create family wealth. What a dynamic way to celebrate family!

I began immediately calculating the possibilities from my family reunion – less than 100 members, meeting biannually for over my lifetime. With just five percent of the spending (airfares, hotels, restaurants, entertainment, car rentals, shopping, etc.) redirected and reinvested into a family corporation would have insured college for all the grandchildren and great grandchild. And with Anderson's vision – a large percentage of this spending can be distributed in our community through our own reunion resorts. This is an idea with merit. This is an idea with muscle for families to build wealth and support our communities.

As an international community developer, I appreciate the research and recognition of the power of the African Diaspora that underlies Anderson's plan. Together, the global African Diaspora can fashion a significant force for economic development. And as the founder/director of a youth mentoring program for global health (Youth Leadership for Global Health, Inc.) I stand with Anderson in placing health, education and economic literacy at the foundation for strengthening families and family reunions.

Anderson, I cheer for you and your far-reaching vision for families of our communities. May Economics as a Second Language meet and exceed all expectations. Watch out, world! This book; this concept is a major step toward "building wealth, one family reunion at a time". This book is dedicated to the memory of Milton Hitchcock and Guy Marbury.

Wilma Ardine Kirchhofer, MPH, Ph.D.

Atlanta, Georgia

INTRODUCTION

" To be a poor man in a land of dollars is hard, but to be a poor race in a land of dollars is the very bottom of hardships" This quote taken from the Souls of Black Folks, written by W.E.B Du Bois in 1903, captures the dilemma with which we have struggled throughout the entire 20th Century. Dr. Du Bios goes on to state that the problem of the 20th century is the problem of the color line. I must insist that the problem of the 21st century then, in keeping with this train of thought proposed by Dr, Du Bois, must be the bottom line.

Of the few avenues that are available for upward economic mobility in America, one has taken a back seat for too long when it is considered by those who want to find solutions to the myriad of problems facing our community. When we consider those avenues, social, cultural, political or economic, we realize that no comprehensive plan has been outlined to deal with the development of the African American community along economic lines.

Economics as a Second Language (ESL) is being put forward to be used as a jumping off point for discussion of how to pool the financial resources of the black community to begin to address the problems of unemployment and underemployment in our communities. The problems of inadequate housing, lack of educational prowess, hopelessness and alienation, which lends itself to high rates of crime, high teenage pregnancy rates, a drain on the public coffers through repeat generations of Black people subsisting on the welfare roles. All of these problems will be addressed and some potential solutions put forward as to how to begin to resolve some of these pressing problems.

What you will find most unique about the solutions that will be proposed is that they will not rely upon Government programs. Nor will they rely upon the philanthropy of individuals of good will, but will concentrate on some institutions already present within our community, as well as the creation of some new institutions to speak to specific areas of concern and welfare within the Black community as a whole. Some solutions will require the formalization of gatherings already being held within the Black community, such as family reunions. The role of the Black church as a potential leader in the development of the economy of the Black community will be discussed.

It is evident to anyone that has studied the Black Community that the Church is by far the oldest and largest institution within the Black community. The majority of Black people in America are Baptist, but Methodist, Protestants, Catholics, and the Islamic religion have made sufficient inroads in the Black community in order to warrant them being considered when we speak of the role of the Black Church in the community.

On any given Sunday, you can find millions of African Americans coming together to worship and to socialize. This must be taken one step further in the quest to legitimize a sense of Black economic empowerment, which has to be developed before we can actualize the pooling of resources. There is clearly a trend toward reaching out to the larger Black community on the part of the Black church through economic development, but it must be given some sort of formalized structure. That is what we are going to propose that we do through the establishment of the Institute for Economics as a Second Language, Inc. (IESL)

The Black Church is by far the richest institution in the Black community and must be urged to use its resources to drag the community as a whole into the arena of economic development in a concerted way. Nothing short of an all out war on poverty, fought from within the community by the black church can free our community from the chains of economic malaise.

While working in the Barrios of California, I was introduced to the concept of ESL, or English as a second language. The theory was put forward by the Hispanic community, and rightly so, that it is impossible to participate fully in the bounty of America, if you are not able to community through the dominant language of the culture which is, of course, English.

Within this concept was hidden the gem of Economics as a Second Language, which speaks more directly to a disenfranchisement that is not only perceived, but is real. According to the vast number of people of color in America who have been locked out of the system for too long, disenfranchisement is the state of their nation.

ESL states that regardless of what your primary language is, whether it is, Spanish, Polish, Italian, or one of the many street dialects prevalent throughout our cities, it is critical that you speak and understand the language and the concepts of economics.

In a society in which capitalism is the order of the day, not to be conversant in the concepts of the free enterprise system is tantamount to perpetual enslavement within the system. ESL begins the process of breaking down the language barriers that prohibit one from functioning effectively within the system. It is a necessity that the language of economics becomes second nature in regards to our relationship with this system.

In America there are two distinct segments of society. Either we are consumers or producers. It is necessary for Black people to become producers. The focus of ESL has to begin early in life and has to continue throughout ones lifetime. We will discuss in this book several suggestions as to how the language of economics can be developed, instituted and ingrained into the upcoming generations of young people, especially in the black community.

It is estimated that in America, there are between 1.5 and 2 million family reunions that take place every year, and that on these reunions nearly 7 billion dollars is spent. The potential surrounding these events will only increase over the course of the next decade. One of our major focuses must be on how to chronicle the already existing family reunions, as well as how to spur the growth of family reunions throughout the nation. It is estimated that family reunions, by the end of this century, could conceivably cover about 80 percent of the Black people in America.

The Black Family Reunion Registry (BFRR) will be developed as a needed tool for the comprehensive development of the program of ESL. The BFRR will be a computerized listing of family reunions, with contact persons throughout America, which would be used to move forward the concept of Family Corporations and Foundations.

Family Corporations and Foundations would be the remaining element of a cohesive, well-rounded potentially revolutionary approach to dealing with the totality of the disenfranchisement of the Black community in terms of economic development.

To capsulate the different elements that will come together to form the basis of the Wealth Network, we have developed the Institute for Economics as a Second language, Inc. IESL will be charged with "Researching and Advocating Health, Education and Economic Literacy through Family Reunions"

Under IESL researchers have developed the curriculum, lesson plan and program development for the teaching of ESL on several different levels. Secondly, the Black Family Reunion Registry will be charged with creating a database of Family Reunion information. Thirdly, a department for research and data collection concerning Family Corporations will be set up and fourthly, the role of the Black Church in moving the Black community into the twenty first century on an equal economic footing within the context of the American free enterprise system will be codified.

Another one of the major components of the Wealth Network was the development of the ESL as a teaching mechanism for young people. The Institute as a non-profit entity that would be responsible for the development of a curriculum, lesson plan and program, that would be taken into elementary, secondary, and high schools to begin the process of teaching young Black children the language of economics.

The institute would also go to the reunions and plan and coordinate sessions for the young members attending those family reunions. This would be done simultaneously with the workshops that would be held for those adult members of the family that would be in attendance. This would give the youth of the family a sense of contribution to the overall development of the business expertise of the family.

HISTORICAL ANALYSIS

The history of Black people in America spans the era of slavery, through emancipation, to the present. As is related in (Black Families in White America, 1968, pg. 27) three facts of Black history must be taken into consideration. First, "Black people came to this country from Africa and not from Europe." Secondly, some came in chains, and were uprooted from their cultural moorings, while others were already here as free men and women (Moorish Americans). Thirdly, they have been subjected to systematic exclusion from participation and influence in the major institutions of this society, even to the present time." This means that Black people have at least been thrice removed from control of the methods of relationship which had been ingrained in their systems in Africa.

Black people had long histories of community and family ties in their systems in Africa prior to being sold into slavery. In (The Black Extended Family, Elmer P. and Joanne Martin, 1978, pg. 94) state that "what slavery did to traditional African Family life was temporarily to minimize extended family ties, breakdown the sense of community found in tribal life, and alienate Africans from authentic identity with their God, their land, and their people." The solution to the total disenfranchisement on the part of Black people must address this all encompassing destruction of character that has taken place. The Family Corporation concept goes a long way toward renewing this sense of kinship.

Plantation life further destroyed the relationship of Blacks by totally destroying the patriarchal family structure. Both Black men and women were treated equally as subservient to the white man who became their father figure.

At this point the nucleus of Black Family life began to be reshaped by assigned relationships between Black men and women, who were brought together by the slave master primarily for the purpose of procreation. Further helping to strengthen whatever sense of community and family life that they felt, was the common plight of all slaves.

Many factors worked against Black people to get them in a position of subservience following emancipation. The sharecropping system, while allowing for some semblance of standards and offered little opportunity to escape the life of poverty. The Martin's relate (The Black Extended Family, 1978, pg. 94) that "The Freedman's Bureau, an organization established by the government, marked the beginning of extensive governmental intervention into Black Family life." This governmental intervention is still in effect today. Although the bureau had little affected on the level of poverty evident in Black Families, it did a great deal to take away control from the family themselves. The ultimate method, through which Black families survived, was the interdependence that developed between extended family members.

Industrialization was another key in the development of the Black nuclear and extended families. Black people had limited opportunity to compete for jobs. Racism played a large part in this, as did the fact that Black people were much more accustomed and trained for agricultural positions. Black families continued and even increased their dependence on governmental aid.

CHAPTER ONE
(Family Reunion Survey Report)

This report presents the results of a survey conducted by the Institute for Economics as a Second Language during the period May 1995 through May 1996. The survey had several goals. One was to gain insight into the market for family reunion services. Second, was to begin compiling two very essential national databases – the Black Family Reunion Registry and the Black Church Registry.

The Institute for Economics as a Second Language (ESL) the non-profit arm of WEALTH NETWORK is dedicated to the development of a strategy to utilize the Church and Family as centers of wealth creation in the African American community. The philosophy of the Wealth Network is focused on the development of financial and investment strategies in the African American community. The Wealth Network through its non profit arm, IESL is also developing an accredited Academy to educate the community in the specialized language, skills and knowledge of financial, investment and economic strategies through family reunions.

The Wealth Network was conceived of in the State of Ohio in 1995. The mission of the Wealth Network is to posture churches and families as practitioners of the philosophy of Economics as a Second Language, and as owners of family reunion lodges. The Wealth Network is positioning itself, through its private profit making arm, Juneteenth Industries, Inc. to establish and dominate the family reunion industry as the number one provider of products and services to this potential billion dollar market.

Mr. Daniel Berry, the associate director of the George Gund Foundation, provided an initial $10,000.00 grant to fund this research project. With their generous assistance, the preliminary survey instrument was developed and data collection commenced on Memorial Day 1995 at the National Council of Negro Women's (NCNW's) Family Reunion Celebration.

Nearly 400 surveys were collected. Survey findings show that 84% of all survey respondents participate in family reunions with interesting variations between metropolitan areas. For example, Metropolitan Washington D.C. shows the highest percentage of family reunion participation and Metropolitan Los Angeles, the lowest.

Forty-six percent (46%) attend reunions at the 2-100 attendance level. Sixteen percent (16%) of all respondents do not attend their family reunions. On average survey respondents spend about $1, 000 per reunion including lodging, travel, food drink, tours, entertainment, and memorabilia and shopping. Findings suggest a correlation between church affiliation and level of participation in family reunions. Fifty–six (56%) percent of respondents reported a place of worship and 44% did not. The church denomination most commonly represented is Baptist as 42% of those who reported a place of worship.

Juneteenth Industries, Inc. (JTI) a Wealth Network subsidiary is devoted to providing quality family reunion services. Specifically, JTI, Inc. plans, coordinates and hosts family reunions, and festivals including related services such as travel, tours, entertainment, memorabilia and local transportation. JTI, Inc. successfully coordinated its first family reunion in July 1996 in Beachwood, Ohio.

Surveys were conducted in seven major metropolitan areas: Cleveland, Ohio; Los Angeles, California; Washington, D.C., Atlanta, Georgia, New York, New York, San Antonio, Texas, and Indianapolis, Indiana. Respondents were solicited from among church groups and fairgoers at the National Council of Negro Women's National Black Family Reunion Celebrations, being held in those cities.

The family-friendly atmosphere of these popular celebrations set a qualitative tone that was compatible with the survey topic. It was anticipated that family-oriented individuals would be attracted to this type of event and would be likely to invest time in activities such as their family reunions.

The survey instrument (or survey form) first requests the name, address and telephone number of the individual filling out the survey (the respondent). For purposes of this report, the term survey will refer to the survey instrument, as well as, to the type of research project.

Question No. 1 asked: Are you a contact person for your family's reunion? It was anticipated that the family reunion contact person would be in the position to make a decision regarding the use of a business such as Juneteenth Associates.

Question No. 2 asked: How many people generally attend your family's reunions? Reponses regarding family reunion size indicate the level of services that might be demanded by potential customers of Juneteenth Associates. If no category was selected it was interpreted that the respondent does not/did not attend his/her family reunions.

Question No. 3 asked: How much money do you estimate that you spend on the following events associated with your family reunion? Eight categories of reunion related spending are delineated. They are: travel, lodging, food, drink, tours, entertainment, memorabilia, shopping and other.

Question No. 4 requested respondents to: Please identify your place of worship. Be as specific as possible. Church Affiliated will be used to refer to respondents who named a place of worship. The Black Family Reunion Registry and The Black Church Registry databases developed from these responses are being maintained and utilized as resources for further research by ESL.

In addition, to the seven main metropolitan areas (Cleveland, Washington D.C., Los Angeles, and Atlanta, San Antonio, Indianapolis and New York, another category "Other Metropolitan Areas" (or "Other Metro") was designated. This category includes surveys completed by respondents from disparate cities in various states. The "Overall" category which is used sometimes includes all survey responses. Other variables, such as, levels of reunion attendance, and church affiliation have been analyzed relative to metropolitan areas.

The Washington D.C. data set includes responses form the standard Metropolitan Washing6ton D.C. area plus those from metropolitan Baltimore, Maryland although the actual standard metropolitan Washington D.C. area does not include Baltimore.

Findings & Analysis

A. Metropolitan Areas Surveyed

A total of 381 surveys were collected from 7 major metropolitan areas. Washington, D.C. contributed 36% of the surveys. Cleveland was represented by 17% and Cincinnati as well was represented by 17% of the surveys. Los Angeles contributed 12% of the surveys and Atlanta, 10%. Eight percent of the surveys represented a variety of cities such as Harrisburg, Pennsylvania, Miami, Florida, and Brooklyn, New York.

Table 1

Surveys Collected By Metro Areas		
Metropolitan Areas	**Percent Of Total**	**Number Received**
Washington D.C.	36%	136
Indianapolis	17%	66
Cleveland	17%	63
Los Angeles	12%	47
Atlanta	10%	40
Other Metro Areas	8%	29

B. Family Reunion Attendance

Overall, 84% of all survey respondents reported that they attend family reunions. Level of reunion attendance is concentrated in the 2-100 range at 48%; with a considerable amount of 26% in the 101-249 range. This equals a total of 72% of reunion attendance reported in these two ranges (2-100/101-249). Of the remaining respondents, 8% reported they attend reunions in the 250-500 categories and 2% reported reunions in the 500 and above category. Lastly, 16% reported they do not attend their family reunions.

Table 2

Overall Reunion Attendance	
Attendance Categories	**% of Total Responses**
2-100	**48%**
101-249	**26%**
250-500	**8%**
500 & above	**2%**
No reunion attendance	**16%**

Attendance and Metropolitan Areas

Reunion attendance findings for specific metropolitan areas range from the highs of 88% for Washington, D.C. and 87% for Other Metropolitan Areas, to a low of 64% for Metropolitan Los Angeles. This represents a 24% difference between the highest and the lowest reunion attendance rates. Other attendance rates are within a close range showing Atlanta at 83%, Cleveland at 80% and Cincinnati at 79%.

Table 3

Reunion Attendance By Metropolitan Area		
Metropolitan Areas	**Attend Reunions**	**Do Not Attend Reunions**
Washington D.C.	88%	12%
Other Metropolitan	87%	13%
Atlanta	83%	17%
Cleveland	80%	20%
Indianapolis	79%	21%
Los Angeles	64%	36%

The highest percentage of respondents by metropolitan area who do not attend family reunions is 36% for Los Angeles. It can be theorized that many Los Angeles residents are inconveniently or intentionally distanced from their root families making reunion attendance less feasible.

Table 4

Reunion Attendance By Attendance Levels and Metropolitan Areas					
Metropolitan Areas	**2-100**	**101-249**	**250-500**	**500 & above**	**Do not Attend Reunions**
Cleveland	52%	18%	6%	5%	19%
Indianapolis	43%	29%	6%	2%	20%
Washington D.C.	51%	26%	10%	1%	12%
Atlanta	45%	25%	10%	2%	18%
Los Angeles	43%	13%	4%	4%	36%
Other Metro	27%	53%	7%	0%	13%
Overall	48%	26%	8%	2%	16%

C. Reunion Related Spending

Sixty-six percent of all survey respondents indicated reunion related spending. The average amount spent on related expenses was $950. Respondents who spent in 4 or more categories (i.e., travel, lodging, food, and drink) spent an average of $1,100 each. Respondents who spent in 3 or less categories spent an average of $780 each. Of those who reported reunion related expenses 60% indicated travel expenses and 45% indicated spending for lodging. Further, the table shows that 55% indicated spending for food, 39% spent on drinks, 15% spent on tours, and 29% on entertainment. Findings also indicate that 25% of respondents who reported reunion related expenses spent on memorabilia, 28% spent on shopping and 12% spent on "'other" expenses. Some of the items listed by respondents in the "other" related expenses category included: postage, long distance phone charges, family gifts, t-shirts, reunion vides, registration fees and family dues.

Table 5

Reunion Related Spending			
	Spending Categories	**Percent of Respondents Who Spend**	**Percent of Total Survey Population**
1.	Travel	60%	40%
2.	Lodging	45%	30%
3.	Food	55%	36%
4.	Drink	39%	26%
5.	Tours	15%	10%
6.	Entertainment	29%	19%
7.	Memorabilia	25%	16%
8.	Shopping	28%	19%
9.	Other	12%	8%

The following table shows expenses by combined spending categories. Findings indicate that 88% of respondents, who reported spending, spend on travel and lodging and an average of $570 was spent. It is further indicate that 80% of respondents, who reported spending, spent for food and drink, at an average of $330 per person. Forty-eight percent (48%) of respondents, who reported spending, spend on entertainment and tours and spend an average of $300. Fifty-eight (58%) of respondents who reported related spending, spend on m3emorabilia and shopping and spend an average of $360. Respondents who spend in the other category, equal 10% of those who reported spending and they spend an average of $160.

Table 6

Spending: Combined Categories and Average Spending		
Spending Categories	**Percent Who Spend**	**Average Spent Per Respondent**
Travel & Lodging	88%	$570
Food & Drink	80%	$330
Entertainment & Tours	48%	$200
Memorabilia & Shopping	58%	$260
Other	10%	$160

D. Church Affiliation

The Black Church is a conduit for a substantial amount of wealth within the Black community is also a major focus of ESL. Due to the number of members represented, level of organization and breadth of influence, churches are targeted for implementation of the ESL principles including family reunion coordinating services by Juneteenth Associates. When church groups are taught to utilize basic financial investment techniques and economic development strategies, the economic wealth of churches and its communities can be turned around.

Church Affiliation by Metropolitan Area

Our findings show that overall, 48% of survey respondents reported a place of worship and 52% did not. The highest rate of church affiliation was reported by Indianapolis at 64 percent. Washington D.C. and Cleveland are not far behind with reported church affiliation rates of 61% and 59% respectively.

The lower church affiliation rates for Atlanta, 53% and other Metropolitan areas, 48%, offer a slight contrast to the Indianapolis, Cleveland and Washington D.C. rates. The church affiliation rate for Los Angeles is the lowest at 40% --approximately 20% lower than rates for Washington, D.C. and Cleveland.

Table 7

Church Affiliation By Metropolitan Areas	
Metropolitan Areas	**Church Affiliated**
Indianapolis	**62%**
Washington, D.C.	**61%**
Cleveland	**59%**
Atlanta	**40%**
Other Metro Areas	**48%**
Los Angeles	**40%**

Church Affiliation and Reunion Attendance

Church affiliated respondents who attend family reunions by metropolitan area range from the highest of the 100% for Other Metropolitan Areas to the lowest of 79% for Los Angeles. Table G compares differences in reported reunion attendance between three categories: Church Affiliated, All (Survey) respondents and Non-Church Affiliated. All Respondents Who Attend is a combined category which includes those who reported a place of worship and those who did not. Although the main focus is between the Church Affiliated and non-church affiliated categories, the All Respondents category simply provides another angle for looking at the information. Generally, the findings show that reunion attendance is higher among those who are associated with a church, and lower among those who are not.

A comparison of reunion attendance for Church Affiliated and Non-Church Affiliated respondents shows a significant difference for all metropolitan areas except Indianapolis. Indianapolis shows only a 5% difference between Church Affiliated (at 92%) and Non-Church Affiliated respondents at (87%). The higher percentage differences are: 38% for both Cleveland and Washington D.C., 25% Los Angeles, 20% Other Metropolitan Areas, and 16% for Atlanta. These represent substantial contrasts between the two categories.

In another instance, a result for Cincinnati is anomalous. Again, in contrast to most metropolitan areas, Cincinnati's Non-Church Affiliated respondents (at 87%) attend reunions at a higher rate than those in the All Respondents category (at 79%).

Table G

Reunion Attendance And Church Affiliation			
Metropolitan Areas	Church Affiliated Who Attend Reunions	Percent of All Respondents Who Attend Reunions	Non-Church Affiliated Who Attend Reunions
Other Metro Areas	100%	87%	80%
Cleveland	97%	80%	59%
Washington	93%	88%	55%
Indianapolis	92%	79%	87%
Atlanta	90%	83%	74%
Los Angeles	79%	64%	54%

E. Church Denominations

Baptist is the largest church denomination represented in the survey. Forty-three percent (43%) of respondents who reported a place of worship are Baptists.

The "Other Denominations" category was designated for churches that did not specify a denomination. Other Denominations claimed as many as 24% of those who named a place of worship. Names of some of those churches included in this category are: New Life Community, Our Redeemer, Mount Olive, New Jerusalem, Innerlight Fellowship, Solid Rock, Mission Revival and Celebration House.

AME churches make up 12% and Catholic churches make up 8% of respondents naming a place of worship. The Islamic Centers and United Methodists comprise 3% each. The Episcopalian and Presbyterian churches account for 2% each and the remaining six denominations, at less than 1% each comprise the remaining 3% of the church denominations reported.

Table H

CHURCH DENOMINATIONS		
1.	BAPTIST	43%
2.	OTHER	24%
3.	AME	12%
4.	CATHOLIC	8%
5.	ISLAMIC	3%
6.	UNITED METHODIST	3%
7.	EPISCOPAL	2%
8.	PRESBYTERIAN	2%
9.	CHURCH OF GOD IN CHRIST	
10.	JESUS CHRIST LATTER DAY SAINTS	
11.	JEHOVAH'S WITNESSES	
12.	LUTHERAN	
13.	METHODIST AME	
14.	SALVATION ARMY	3%

F. <u>Summary</u>

These results indicate the majority of the survey population participates in family reunions. Further, they give a profile of several aspects of the African-American community. Namely, the extent to which African-American families engage in family reunions, the average amount of money spent related to family reunions, and the extent to which African-Americans are affiliated within the church community. The need to understand the current status of Black families and churches and the need to develop both as institutions adept in economics and wealth creation is critical.

With the advent of high technology, Black Families have been dealt an even more significant setback in their hopes for more access to the means of economic fulfillment so necessary to the development and maintenance of strong nuclear and extended families.

To date nearly 6,000 family reunion use surveys have been compiled and the data base is being built to accommodate this information. IESL now has the most extensive data base of information related to the spending power connected with black family reunions in the world. This information will soon be available to be scrutinized by scholars and others interested in culling trends and opportunities that might be inherent for marketing to this population.

This is a copy of the actual survey that has been developed and outlines the questions that have allow IESL to become a primary repository of data relating to the economic spending power inherent in the family reunion movement in America.

CHAPTER TWO
(SOCIOLOGICAL BACKGROUND)

Primitive communism is the oldest form of sociological structure known in Africa. It outlines a system in which the tribe or community is broken down into groups whose assignments are to hunt, gather, farm, etc. The rewards for this labor are to be shared with the community as a whole. This to a large extent was the system in place prior to the coming of slavery to West Africa. This changed dramatically once Black people were brought to America.

The extended family was the dominant structure of family life during the pre-slavery period. The extended family was a "Multigenerational, Interdependent Kinship System" (The Black Family, Elmer P. and Joanne Martin, 1978, pg. 45) and according to this theory, the extended family can do little to help its members become full participants in urban society. However, it is a powerful mechanism for assuring basic needs and for giving its m members a sense of solidarity.

Mr. Harvey Hunter, a Southern California restaurant owner authored a book entitled "The Scientific Definition of God" in which he asserts that the "Black Extended Family" is a reality by virtue of our birth. Mr. Harvey declares in his book that "The Black Extended Family" is not an organization; it is the spiritual birth-right of all descendants of slaves in America, and by extension, around the world. It sustained our forefathers, according to him, and saw them through the darkest night of cruel, inhuman bondage; and they have passed this legacy on to us.

Mr. Harvey goes on to state that "The Black Extended Family" will break the shackles of drugs, gangs, violence, poverty and hopeless deprivation, and will bring us collective and individual wealth, and success beyond our wildest imagination.

The Wealth Network through its many organizations is dedicated to the elimination of a poverty mindset and the implantation of wealth consciousness through family reunions. IESL, along with Juneteenth Industries, Inc. Ghenmor Import/Export Trading Co., the Black Family Reunion Registry and Rough Gem Auction .com forms a network around and through which family corporations can invest in themselves and each other and provide a perfect format for securing capital and assets for future generations.

In America the nuclear family became the dominant pattern for family relationships and was much more difficult for Black people to assimilate into because it requires a certain amount of self-sufficiency. The traditional African life was patriarchal, polygamous, communal and tribal, and was organized around elaborate kinship ties. (Elmer P. and Joanne Martin, 1978, pg. 93) The question before us in modern times is how we can as Black people overcome obstacles to become self-sufficient in a nuclear and extended family concept. Black people have begun to rely less on their own survival mechanisms and community support networks and more and more on the government and on their own personal mechanisms without much overall success.

How can Black people build the kind of community solidarity necessary to guarantee a role in determining how successful they will be in terms of moving into the twenty first century? The time to begin to address these concerns is now. The family corporation concept, grown out of family reunions, offers us this mechanism. Economics as a Second Language Incorporated provides such a mechanism for carrying out the institutionalization of Family reunions.

In the Souls of Black Folks, by W.E.B Du Bois he states, "The socioeconomic truth as he sees it is that, just as African Americans under the corporate rule of monopolized wealth ...will be confined to the lowest wage group, so the peoples of the developing world face subordination in the global scheme of things capitalist. Black folks insulating themselves in protected city enclaves and distant suburbs, and the rise of Black Republicanism, the prospects of the poor and the dark skinned in deindustrializing America are likely to become ever more Malthusian as their potential leadership is creamed off and alienated from them.

True leadership for overcoming the pitfalls to self determination must come from the community where a majority of African Americans find themselves trapped. We must transform that trap ness into the very thing that gives up the ability to liberate ourselves. Instead of fighting against one another for an ever shrinking slice of the pie, we must use our numbers to create more pies from which to eat.

In his book "Winning the Economic Development Championship" Erbie Phillips Jr. argues that there is clear and incontrovertible evidence that the pie is indeed increasing in size, and that the best way to measure that growth and development is over a longer period of time. The best reason to use longer time frames as a measure of growth is that economic activity fluctuates over a shorter period of time.

According to Mr. Phillips, and I agree, studies show that millions of African Americans are better off today that they were twenty years ago. Contrary to all negative reports, many African Americans have improved their standards of living considerably.

STATISTICS ON AFRICAN AMERICAN ECONOMIC GROWTH:

- ❖ $1 to $2499, represented 41 percent of African Americans during 1967; while in 1991 the percentage was 22.5. A change that represented a reduction of 18.5 percent in the number of African Americans earning that amount of income.

- ❖ $2500 to 4999, 33.5 percent during 1967; while in 1991 the percentage was 27.4. A change that reflected a reduction of 6.1 percent.

❖ $5000 to $9999, 39.6 percent during 1967; while in 1991 the percentage was 45.1, a growth of 5.5 percent in this category. It is safe for me to assume that 5.5% of the 24.6% from the lowest income levels moved into this category, additionally this means that 19.1% of these individuals moved even higher.

❖ $10000 to $14999, 30.4 percent during 1967, while in 1991 the percentage was 28.3. A change that represents a reduction of 2.1%.

❖ The statistics show that 21.1% of these individuals earned more than $15,000 in 1991 than in 1991.

African Americans as a group still earn less income than the national average, even though some African Americans are experiencing substantial economic growth. This growth must not be taken for granted because progressive African Americans have experienced a greater economic growth rate than White Americans. Over the twenty four year prior ending in 1991, the per capita income (which is an important factor used to measure economic growth) of whites had grown 59%, and for African Americans 74%. This difference represents a plus 15% gain for African Americans.

The key then becomes how we can use the benefits from this economic growth to develop a solid and formidable economic base. I submit to you that it is necessary for us to look at the travel and tourism industry, through family reunions as an opportunity for investing these profits for future generations.

In order to increase the benefits gained from the increase in this economic spending power it is necessary to increase the production of products and services coming from our community and increase the level of jobs being provided as a result of this increase. As is stated in "Winning the Economic Development Championship" accomplishing the goals of increased production will also require an increase in ownership of the "Factors of Production" These "factors" are the back-bone or foundation for the economy of any group, society, or nation, according to Mr. Erbie Phillips. The factors of production include, land, capital, labor, and entrepreneurship

Purchasing more "Factors of Production" is very important to any group if they are to have long term economic development. To acquire the "Factors of Production" a group needs investment. African Americans must increase their own sources of venture capital by combining their financial resources and pooling their assets. What better way to accomplish this goal, than through family reunions.

CHAPTER THREE
(The Family Corporation Concept)

The family corporation concept deals with the empowerment of the Black community through economic development. The two schools of thought prevalent today suggest that the reasons that Black people are disenfranchised in America can be traced back to societal roadblocks that have been placed in the paths of individuals of African Descent; such as a lack of affordable housing, inferior education and limited access to decent jobs. Still others are of the "blame the victim" school of thought, which declares that the blame falls squarely on the shoulders of Black people themselves and a breakdown of the Black Family unit.

Both arguments have some merit, but what we fail to realize is that both the family and society are composed of individuals who have interdependence. Especially in the Black community, these networks must be brought to bear on the tremendous problems that we now face.

Family reunions are becoming commonplace in the Black community with large numbers of relatives gathering yearly. Renewing old acquaintances; making new ones and introducing younger family members to their relatives for the first time. What ESL Incorporated proposes to do is to harness all of this energy and to turn it into a business opportunity for the entire community. These reunions must be used for more than just social gatherings, where after the reunions are over another year passes with only minimal contact between the participants being maintained. Through the BFRR we will maintain an ongoing contact between individuals interested in the family reunion movement and various different family reunions.

The Family Corporations concept envisions the Family reunion as the fulcrum upon which families and society can be transformed into networks for development and advancement in all areas critical to the growth and survival of its members. Here the extended and nuclear families come together like at no other point, or time. As a result of this coming together, offer an excellent opportunity to address and find solutions to the most fractious problems that face society in general, and Black families in particular. Such as, the lack of role models and the formation of support networks to provide incentive where none previously existed.

From a historical and sociological perspective, we hope to show that the Family Corporation Concept is the next logical step in the development of the Black Family unit through decades and centuries of slavery, reconstruction, Jim Crowism, to Black empowerment and beyond. How can we as black people utilize this most precious resource- the family reunion- to raise the level of participation in all aspects of the American way of life; from spiritual to economic, from education to personal achievement?

Included at the back of this book are all the forms needed in order to establish a family corporation around your family reunion, and to begin the process of pooling the resources represented yearly at the gathering of your family unit. This forms are accompanied by a CD Rom which contains all the relevant information needed to fill out the paperwork and submit it so that your family can them be represented by a board of directors elected at your family reunions to conduct the business of your family corporation.

Not only will you find all of the necessary forms, but you will find a comprehensive approach to submitting all of the paperwork. Once you have decided to become a part of the revolutionary new movement. You can fill out an application to become a member of IESL at a level which will give you unlimited access to counselors, both financial and legal, who will assist you in all aspects of developing a fully functional family corporation.

It is the objective of IESL to bring together 10,000 family corporations into cooperative organization that can be used to facility wealth development, asset accumulation and economic empowerment on a level here-to-fore unforeseen in the annals of community economic empowerment.

CHAPTER FOUR
(WHY INCORPORATE AS A FAMILY?)

The propitiation and well being of the family offers us the best reason for why the family unit should be used as a central focus for a corporation. There is in the development of a business, the necessity to bring together people who are like minded in terms of what they want to get out of a business venture. In the case of the Family Corporation Concept the motivation is dual in nature. First and foremost, it is to move the family ahead in terms of providing for its members, and second, it is the motivation toward profit, which could be used for a number of things. For instance, the profit could be used to help strengthen the family through the provision of adequate housing and educational opportunities. If the motive is profit alone, which often the case in business, you are left open to the whims of greed. The adage, that there is strength in numbers, can be related to the family as a unit. So you have the interest for being successful and the ability to pool resources, along with a certain amount of admiration and trust. What is missing in this equation is simply the knowledge needed to make it work.

Black people can increase the success rate of businesses by increasing the social support network system available to them. The extended family offers the perfect mechanism for providing this network. Black family reunions often bring together in excess of three hundred extended family members and friends. What better place then to utilize this power and strength than in the development of a mechanism which can tap into the financial infrastructure of America, in order to increase the success rate of members of the family unit and therefore the extended family as a whole?

Many of the family members have to some extent been involved in some form of business development, and have gained expertise which could be used to bring together acceptable business plans and loan packages, not to mention the provision of role models for success.

The one area of life which has suffered the most in the development of the Black Extended Family has been the denial of access to capital. When the opportunities were most ripe for reaping the rewards of American free enterprise; periods such as the land rushes, gold strikes, and development of industrial conglomerates; Black people were being denied equal opportunity. At the present time most of the natural resources of the country, upon which wealth to a certain extent is based, are already in the hands of others. Wealth and power have been passed for centuries down through generations. When you are born into money it makes life a great deal easier.

According to paper written by Dr. Michael Sherraden entitled "Rethinking social Welfare: Towards Assets", it is necessary for America to begin to rethink its policy toward poverty and redirect it away from income maintenance of the poor in America and toward asset accumulation. Dr. Sherraden puts forward the proposition, with which I agree, that "Assets refer to the stock of wealth in a household – net assets or net worth. In contrast, income refers to the flow of resources in a household, a concept associated with consumption of goods and services and standard of living. These are the two most fundamental financial concepts, illustrated in accounting by two basic types of financial reports, income statements and balance sheets. In this regard, social welfare policy has been constructed almost exclusively in terms of household income statements rather than in terms of household balance sheets.

Wealth is not income, spending and consumption, but rather savings, investment, and assimilation of assets. As much as 60 percent of the poverty population are more likely to be children, Black, rural, and live in the south and reside in families headed by single female heads of household or are headed by elderly.

Dr. Sherraden states "that the idea of income, from employment or any other source while obviously extremely important provides an inadequate foundation from which to interpret social welfare problems and construct potential solutions." The census of 1980 states that the richest 5 percent of Americans receive about the same income as the bottom 40 percent, but the richest 1 percent own a many assets as the bottom 90 percent.

Among all households, equity in a home accounted for 41 percent of net worth. Other significant proportions were in interest-earning assets (17 percent), businesses or professions (10 percent), rental property (9 percent), stocks (7 percents), and vehicles (6 percent). Assets tend to grow larger through age 65, then decline somewhat. Education is positively associated with asset accumulation. Assets are unevenly distributed by race. According to the Census Bureau, in 1984 the median white household had a net worth of $39,135, eight times higher than the $4,913 net worth of the median Hispanic household, and 12 times higher than the $3,397 net worth of the median Black household.

To quote Dr. Sherraden, "the wealthy maintain their assets and pass them along to children not entirely through superior intelligence, particular character traits, or hard work, but through elaborate structures of information, associations, procedures, and favorable rules. In short, they operate within privileged institutions, both public and private, that facilitate asset accumulation, and the process tends to be intergenerational. The vast majority of wealthy people in the United States have inherited their wealth."

To further elaborate on Dr. Sheridan's theory of the significance of assets over income, he goes on to state, "among the upper middle class there are two important forms of asset accumulation: home ownership and retirement pensions. Thus, the upper middle class accumulates its wealth, not so much through superior individual investment, but through structured, institutionalized arrangements that are in many respects difficult to miss. However, structured, institutionalized arrangements that are in many respects difficult to miss. However, for those receiving public assistance, not only is asset accumulation not encouraged, it is not permitted. Without the possibility of asset accumulation, families tend not to plan for a better future and do not accumulate a cushion that might sustain them during a climb out of poverty."

To support the need for the development of Family Corporation, I would like to continue relating briefly some of the literature cited by Dr. Sherraden. "In terms of household stability, the principal role of assets is to cushion income shocks that accompany major illness, job loss, or marital break-up. Nearly every transaction for an impoverished family is more difficult and proportionately more costly, in this way, poverty is actually more expensive, and these expenses keep poor people poor. Assets reduce household transaction cost through direct purchase of more reliable goods and services through access to institutional, rather than household, forms of transaction costs support, thereby shifting the burden from the family to institutions."

In a study by R. E. Paul comparing the lower and middle classes, one striking conclusion is that members of middle-class households not only enjoy more stable employment income, but are also more likely to work in non-employment activities to better the household financial position (home remodeling and maintenance, improving skills). In other words, the presence of higher income and assets is associated with increased non-labor market productivity. A partial explanation of these results is that those with assets have assets to protect, se a more positive future, and consequently are more willing to spend time and energy improving their condition. According to Dr. Sherraden, "this process might be called, "the social construction of future possibilities" and it is, in all likelihood, the primary social-psychological mechanism by which classes are produced."

A well-publicized news story, reflecting the opposite side of the coin, is worth recounting. In 1980, Eugene Lang, a multimillionaire industrialist, gave a commencement address to 61 sixth graders in Harlem. Most were Black or Hispanic. Most were poor. He told them that if they stayed in school, he would pay college tuition for everyone in the class. In 1985, the students were in the 11th grade. All 51 of the students remaining in the New York area had stayed in school, and many were doing well enough to qualify for college.

Two of the nine students who had left the area had stayed in touch with Lang; and they also had stayed in school and planned to go to college. Given the normal dropout rate of up to 50 percent for this population, this record of educational achievement is remarkable. "Several students said they thought that Lang's concept had worked because many children in the neighborhood put ides of college out of their minds at an early age, thinking that it was a luxury beyond their reach."

It is not sufficient nor realistic for us as Black Americans to think that anyone outside of our own sphere of community is going to play Santa Claus for us and so it is necessary that we develop our own mechanism for spurring our children toward higher education and a realization that if they work real hard in school a way will be forthcoming to guarantee them an opportunity for a higher education. The Family Corporation Concept involves just such an incentive.

The Family Corporation Concept begins to address the need for acquiring and holding on to a wealth that is familial in nature and not individual. When taken individually, the resources available within the Black community might not seem sufficient to break out of the cycle of poverty. But if pooled into a family trust of some kind, resources might be sufficiently strong enough to allow the chains of poverty to be broken and the creation of a new cycle of strong education and financial self-reliance to be put into place.

CHAPTER FIVE
(CAPITAL FORMATION)

As was mentioned above, the accumulation of capital is the largest bonus that could be offered as a result of the Family Corporation Concept. Quite often homes, property, life insurance benefits are held by individual family members, which taken separately don't amount to a great deal, but if pooled could lay the base for a sizeable down payment toward the development of a business concept. If we use the model of some churches, we begin to see that often parishioners, as the result of their beliefs are asked and consent to deed over their valuables and property to the church in order to show their faith.

The family members could decide that as a method of gathering the wealth, that the property which they hold; however meager or extravagant, could be combined to form the basis for a corporation. With shares in the corporation being issued as compensation for the amount of property turned over to the corporation.

Family Corporations would be the exact opposite of Family Foundations that were established to distribute money that had been accumulated. The Corporations would be responsible for the solicitation of funds through grants and awards and the making of profit, to help the extended family in the areas of housing, job creation and education.

The members of the Family Corporation would also be required on a monthly basis to purchase a certain number of shares in the corporation. Three hundred family members contributing to a fund, even a minimal amount of money over the years could accumulate a significant amount of money. Of course, it is not reasonable to assume that every family member is going to be capable of contributing or agreeable to the efficacy of such a plan, but many are going to recognize this is a valuable tool for addressing some of the problems faced by the extended family members. In order to participate in the rewards you must participate in the growth and development of the Family Corporation.

PROFIT/NON PROFIT MODEL

The most critical aspect of the Corporation will be its legal status. The Family Corporation Concept must take two major factors into consideration. The first factor which must be taken into consideration is the welfare and well-being of the extended family members. The second, the creation of profit, which can assist in reaching the first goal, through the awarding to family members of scholarships, the purchase or property, and meeting other expenses of the corporation.

The non profit arm of the corporation in conjunction with the profit making would fit best in filling the age old void that exists within the Black Family community in terms of business development. Some things can best be accomplished in a profit making environment, while others need the non profit atmosphere to be successful. For instance, in order to apply to foundations, you should buy and large be a non profit corporation. But in order to create a corporation which issues stock and creates profit, must you be a private profit making corporation? The answer to that is no. Non Profit corporations can be used as stock corporations, but the difference is that as a not for profit corporation, the profit must be used for the benefit of the corporation as a whole, and not for any individual.

The family reunions that are held annually could become business meetings and could become tax write-off's for the participants. This could be true for a lot of the property that is now being held by individuals within the family. If that same property were owned by a corporation, the flexibility in how to use it for financial gain would be greatly increased. These are all avenues that must be explored by families in order to help lift themselves from throes of poverty.

The ways in which non-profit corporations can work together for mutual benefit are still not clear. There is, however, a current trend toward the utilization of the two to solve a number of intractable problems within the community. This method must be seriously considered by the Family Corporation concept.

THE VOCABULARY OF INVESTING

Some of the concepts that would be dealt with by the Institute would be as follows:

BANKING

Information on banking, such as, don't take the first offer of a loan from a bank. Shopping around or negotiating for a better rate could save you hundreds of dollars in the long run. Don't accept a loan based on rate alone. Make sure that you add in up-front fees and charges and closing costs. This could make the rate that you actually end up paying for a loan more expensive. Make sure that you know whether a rate on the loan is fixed or variable. The latter is better if rates are falling. Right now the odds favor the numbers getting lower, but if they rise in the next year, then at least you would have been warned. You should also find out whether or not the bank might be willing to reduce your rate if you agree to make automatic payments from your checking account, or if you keep other accounts as the same institution. It is also important that you bring proof of income, such as a recent payroll stub, when applying for a loan. Banks are beginning to take a harder look at such things as income and length of residency. And finally, make sure that you re able to repay the loan on time. That includes such factors as job security and other obligations.

CORPORATIONS

Businesses don't have to be "corporations", but when they are, they are like artificial people. They can buy, own and sell property. Corporations can be sued, but their human owners are liable only for what they've invested.

COMMON STOCK – When you own common stock, you own part of corporation. You have the right to vote your shares at the company's annual meeting. The greater the number of shares, the greater your influence is in the company.

PREFERRED- Holders of preferred stock get paid what's due them before common stockholders do. Some stock is non-voting, and other stock has restrictions on ownership.

DIVIDEND- A dividend is money a company pays its shareholders periodically. If you held 100 shares and the dividend was 1.50 per share, you would receive a check for $150.

SPLITS- When a stock splits, it means that the company wants to exchange every $100 share for two $50 shares, ten $10 shares, or some other combination. You get more shares, but not more cash value.

PAR VALUE- Par Value is some arbitrary, assigned value printed on a stock certificate. It means nothing.

BOOK VALUE- Book Value relates to how much a corporation is actually worth. It is calculated by starting with assets – the money, objects, land and other holdings, then subtracting liabilities – debts and other obligations – and finally dividing the answer by the number of shares in the hands of all investors.

MARKET VALUE- Market Value is what a willing buyer would pay now, or the last closing price of the stock.

MARKETS- The term refers to the organized trading of securities through a market called an exchange. America's biggest stock shops are the New York Stock Exchange and the American Stock Exchange, both in New York. There are smaller exchanges in several other cities. Most major countries outside of the United States also have stock exchanges.

BULLS AND BEARS- When stock prices fall for an extended period, it is said to be a "bear" market. When prices rise for an extended period, it is called a "bull" market. No one really knows why.

BONDS - Bondholders lend money to governments or corporations – they are not owners the way stockholders are.

MUTUAL FUNDS – Mutual funds are simply pools of money from many people that are invested in stocks, bonds or other securities.

OPTIONS – Options, popular with speculators, are rights to buy or sell a security at a certain price within a certain time. If you hold an option, you do not have to follow through.

FUTURES – Futures, on the other hand, involve an obligation to buy or sell that security. If you hold a future contract to buy stock on a certain date, you will have to fork over the money on that date unless you can sell the contract to someone else beforehand.

INDEXES - Because millions of securities are in circulation, it would be impossible for investors to keep up each day with all of them. Still, people need a way to determine how their investments are doing. Over time, market-measuring sticks have been created.

 The Dow Jones industrial average, which tracks 30 high-quality stocks as a group, is the most commonly indicator of the stock market's performance. The Dow has closed as high as 2, 99.75

BLUE CHIPS – That's what is in the Dow 30. Basically it means stocks that are considered safe investments likely to show growth over time. The terms come from poker, which should give you a better idea of what investing really is.

BROKERS – In most cases, you buy stocks and bonds, options and futures through a broker. You pay a commission, based on the number of shares traded or the dollar value of the transaction. There are no legal limits on what a broker can charge, so shop around.

SEC- In 1934, the federal government created the Securities and Exchange Commission to act as a watchdog and protect the public. The SEC has jurisdiction over publicly sold securities, the companies that issue them and the brokers who sell them. SEC rules are available in library reference rooms and in many books on investing.

In order to be better informed, stockholders should learn to interpret materials that public companies must make available – annual reports, proxy statements and especially the more detailed 10K report that is filed annually with the SEC.

BONDS

Information on investing in bonds and the variety of different types of investments that are available should be apart of the overall package of financial information that is disseminated to the clients of the institute. We might want to address several different types of bonds and determine which ones will be right for which types of investors. For instance, short-term bond funds can be viewed as highly disciplined with a some what longer portfolio maturity span. Eighty percent of its holdings must be top-rated corporate or Government bonds.

Average maturity of bonds in this fund is about three years, because it expects interest rates to continue falling and it wants to lock in today's yields for a while. This is unlike money funds, which reflect lower rates within a few weeks. Pioneer Bond funds have been rejecting corporate debt in favor government agency mortgage backed issues.

You benefit from professional money management and a diversified portfolio (which usually means less risk) providing the yield is 8.7% which is considered average, your monthly $100 will yield $7, 483.32 in five years; $19, 026 in 10 years.

MONEY MARKET FUNDS

A money market is a type of mutual fund with the advantage of being relatively risk free because the fund's management invests shareholders' money in U.S. government securities, bank certificates of deposit and other short-term debt.

Once you get in the habit of stashing $100 each month, set a goal that when your accumulated savings total certain amount – such as $1,000 – you will invest the money in something that offers an even higher rate of return.

CERTIFICATES OF DEPOSIT

When you buy a certificate of deposit from a bank or other financial institution, you're guaranteed a fixed rate that won't dip, even though rates on other savings plans do. Your opening deposit may be as low as $500 for long-term certificate, more for short-term. Normally, the longer the term, the higher the interest rate is.

HIGHER YIELD INVESTMENTS

When the amount money you have to invest increases, so to does your options, and your opportunities to incur greater rates of return on your investment. The risk potential also increases, of course, so you will need to educate yourself even more and perhaps obtain professional assistance.

U.S. TREASURY SECURITIES

Treasury bills (minimum denominations of $10,000) mature in a year or less; Treasury notes (issued in minimums of $1,000) mature in two to 10 years; and Treasury bonds (similar to notes, but maturity is 10 years or more). They are considered virtually risk-free.

CORPORATE BONDS

Corporate bonds are a way for corporations to borrow money from the general public. These usually pay a fixed interest rate over a fixed term. Interest payments are generally made to the bondholders every six months and at the end of the term the principal is paid back.

PREFERRED STOCKS

Like bonds, these are issued with a designated "par value" and have a specified rate of return. Investors receive dividends. If a company goes broke, preferred stockholders have second claim on its assets, after bondholders – but before holders of common stock.

A WOMENS GUIDE TO RETIREMENT PLANNING

One of the things that must be considered in the Black community is that women greatly outnumber men and must think about securing their own future. At most family reunions you will find that the ratio of women to men, in terms of those that are oldest, is great.

The average age at which a woman is widowed is 56 percent, and married women have an 85 percent chance of facing their later years without a mate. Seventy percent of the older poor are women, and 75 percent of all nursing home residents ages 65 and older are women. The average annual cost of nursing home care is $25,000, while the median income of women over age 60 (including social security and pension) is $6,300.

It is never too early to start saving. In fact, the earlier you start saving, the better. Retirement accounts should be looked at an early age in order to guarantee sufficient income during retirement. Individual retirement accounts are savings or investments accounts that allow you to put money away now for retirement and generally not pay taxes on either the original deposits or the accumulated interest until you withdraw your money before age 59 ½ with paying a penalty tax to the Internal Revenue Service. Some plans let you open and Individual Retirement Account (IRA) with as little as $50.00, and you can add to it weekly, monthly, or yearly. There is a limit of $2,000 (and sometimes less) on how much an individual can contribute to an IRA each year. Similar to an IRA, a Keogh plan is tailored to the self-employed. You are eligible if you own your own business.

SOCIAL SECURITY

Family financial planning should include knowledge of how you and your family are insured under social security. Social Security or FICA taxes are paid by most working people, but few think of the protection Social Security offers for their family during their working years.

We look forward to retirement and know that Social Security benefits will be part of our retirement income; but how many of us realize that our families are protected against loss of income in case of our death or disability?

For example, Lisa worked as a customer service representative for four years until last March when she was in a serious auto accident. Now she is 25 and unable to work due to her condition. Through her job she had been paying Social Security tax. Now, Lisa is receives an additional $350 each month for Tommy, her two year old son. She plans to get career counseling and training for a new career suitable for her present physical limitations. But for now, Lisa and Tommy are secure with a monthly income from Social Security.

Do you know if you are covered in case of disability? Would your family be covered if you were to die? To find out call 1-800-234-5772 and ask to have a Personal Earnings and Benefit Estimate Statement request form sent to you. Then complete that form and mail it to the Social Security Administration address printed on the form. Within a few weeks you will receive a complete record of how much you have paid into Social Security. The reply will also show whether or not you and your family are insured for disability, survivor and retirement benefits and how much the monthly benefit would be for you and your family.

The Personal Earnings and Benefit Estimate Statement is free from the Social Security Administration to anyone under the age of 65 who has worked in Social Security covered employment or self-employment.

These are but a few of the issues that the institute will prepare itself to deal with through curriculum and lesson plan development. The institute will become an indispensable resource within the Black community for dealing with these very much real life issues. In most quarters of the American populace, this information, to a certain extent, is second nature, but in the Black community contained here are questions which are not often if ever considered. The issues outlined above contain the seed of the free enterprise system, and as Black Americans can become familiar with the issues and their ramifications will determine the success for utilizing the system for the fulfillment of long held dreams and desires. Goals of economic freedom are embedded like pearls in their shells in the context of this information, and it will become the objective of the Economics as a Second Language Institute to pry this information from the recesses where it has been long held and impart the same to the Black community where it is so desperately needed.

IESL Inc. would be organized through this regional concept and would be tied into a national database, which would oversee this coordinated effort toward linking individuals of African decent through the family reunions. While we recognize the gigantic nature of the undertaking, we also realize that it is well within the range of the possible and in our way of looking at it; it is an idea whose time has come.

CHAPTER SIX
(EDUCATION/HOUSING/JOBS)

The three gravest problems facing the Black community and the Black family are education, housing and jobs. Any program that seeks to increase on an equitable basis the participation of Black people in the American dream must first address these disparities.

The Family Corporation Concept would be the perfect vehicle for addressing these most grievous faults in the system. The corporation would be designed to purchase property and housing in which family members could live. Educational scholarships could be designed to make sure that all of the youth would have access to a decent education. Once the skills are gained they would be made available to the family at large. Every family needs an attorney, an accountant, a dentist, and a physician. As the result of the scholarship and the support from the Family Corporation that individual, upon completion of their program of training, would be available as a resource for the extended family.

The person receiving support would then pledge to assist other family members in their educational pursuit. Through the creation of small businesses, jobs for stock of the corporation could become the job of the extended family members. Plumbers, electricians, painters, etc., could be trained and hired to make sure that the property is kept in tip top shape. This might all sound too good to be true, but as a long-term project, it could become a reality. We as the Black community have nothing to lose and everything to gain.

It is understood in the Black community, as is succinctly stated in Black families in White America (Andrew Billingsley, 1968, pg. 82), "the ability of Black people to meet the needs of its community members and the functional requirements of society are intimately associated with its position on the socioeconomic pyramid." It's critical we begin to understand the need to take control of our own economic destiny, and not depend on the government or others to guarantee it for us. At that point we will become full and productive members of a society as a whole.

CHAPTER SEVEN
(REPARATIONS)

Whether or not reparations ever become a reality or not, one area that has to be taken into consideration in the family Corporation Concept is the question of how is the government going to inject those funds into the Black community. There is a movement afoot in the Black community, similar to the one that took place in the Japanese community that eventually lead to compensation being paid to each Japanese citizen who suffered from the internment during World War II.

One of the major questions that will be asked is how is this money to be distributed? This way they can guarantee that the funds are used to help raise the level of the Black community as a whole. In order to gain some sort of parity with those segments of the population who benefited either directly or indirectly form the wealth created by the utilization of free slave labor. The Black community must be able to answer that question. I feel that the utilization of the Family Corporation concept founded around Black Family reunions could be the conduit for funneling the funds into the Black community. I think that all families currently experiencing reunions should be encouraged to organize Family Corporations immediately.

Whether you are of the school of thought that ascribes to the principle of blaming society or the Black community for all of the ills of the Black community, we as the Black community must take responsibility for our own extraction from second class citizenship in America. The Family Corporation Concept offers each of us a solution to the factionalism evident throughout society and the Black community specifically, that has held back progress on behalf of Black people for nearly a century and a half, following the termination of chattel slavery. The Family Corporation concept gives us a vehicle for addressing these most pressing problems that are faced by a majority of members of the Black community.

The family has always, with the exclusion of slavery, played a large part in the sociological structure of the Black community, and in spite of the dispersed nature of Black people offers us a method reinvigorating our family relationships like nothing has before. The perils that are faced on the road to fulfillment on behalf of the Black community will be numerous, but in unity there is strength, and in family there is a support network. Capitalism has traditionally been a system in which rugged individualism has been prized and admired. The Family Corporation concept offers capitalism an opportunity to put on a new face, one in which social prosperity is as important as individual financial prosperity. I hope that this concept of Economics as a Second Language may help to contribute toward that end.

CHAPTER EIGHT
(WHY INSTITUTE A FAMILY FOUNDATION?)

There are over 30,000 foundations in the United States, with only 500 of them having been established by minorities, so says Karen Lynn, a member of the Council of Foundations, who was assigned several years ago to chronicle the benevolent traditions of America's Blacks, Hispanics, Asians, and American Indian communities. Increasingly, members of racial and ethnic minorities are creating foundations to help their own people or society in general, reports the Council on Foundations, a resource house for 1,200 grant making organizations.

Foundations have been established by scores of melting pot Americans – like Joe Shoong, a Chinese immigrant merchant; Mary Carmen Saucedo, a Hispanic retired school administrator; or Lonnie Porter, a Black janitor who died at age 93 and left his $100,000 life savings to set up an endowment that supports students at the United Theological Seminary in Payton, Ohio.

Economics as a Second Language Corporation would help to provide Legal Consultations in setting up a Family Foundation in which the family could pool their resources, both financial and material, to further the educational, or health services goals for their extended families. According to the Council of Foundations it requires money, but not a fortune to establish a Foundation. Two thousand dollars can make a full fledged philanthropist, with a fund bearing your family name and perpetuate your good intentions into eternity.

In an article written by Emmett d. Carson entitled "the evolution of Black Philanthropy; Patterns of giving and Voluntarism", he states that the debate is quickening about the need for the Black community to take a more active role in the development and implementation of strategies aimed at helping poor blacks. A variety of factors have provided an impetus for this discussion, including (1) the belief that increasingly fewer routes provide the poor with upward socioeconomic mobility; (2) the growing income disparity between the Black middle class and the Black poor; and (3) a belief by many that the current national budget deficit will effectively prevent any substantial expansion of federal domestic programs to address the needs of the poor. The process by which this self help was to occur has been lacking, but with the focus on family reunions, a way has been found to initiate this plan. Middle class Black family members have a natural tendency to want to reach back and pull poorer family members along. At each reunion one thing becomes clear that most extended families members along. At each reunion one thing becomes clear that most extended families cover the gamut in terms of where they come from on the socioeconomic scale.

In the report written by Karen Lynn she states "looking beyond the perception of minorities as the recipients of charity, you will find these communities have always been benevolent. Black people have a tradition of selfless giving dating back many centuries. "Giving, and not receiving, marks the histories of these minority groups."

In the United States there are over 30,000 foundations, with assets of over 122 billion dollars. In 1988, they gave away $7.4 billion. Having a foundation removes a lot of pressure; it allows people to feel that they can give to charity in a methodical, logical way without being inundated by request.

Some minority foundations have assets of as little as $25,000. What makes a charity a foundation is the way it is set up. With a pool of money that is invested, with earnings given away, but the endowment remaining and generating more income for the founders there are substantial tax benefits to be gained.

In 1852, William Lloyd Garrison observed that "He was encouraged to find not only among Black Bostonians, but in other cities, a disposition to form societies, both among men and women, for mutual improvement and assistance." A review of Black Americans indicates that Blacks historically have relied on the philanthropic resources of their own community to provide for the Black poor as well as to supply the people the financial resources to sustain virtually every Black protest movement throughout history. Economics as a Second Language could possibly be the next major social and economic movement to take place in America. It is fair to assume that the Black community would be very supportive of such a concept.

An early example of Black philanthropic activity being utilized as public power was the Underground Railroad. In recounting the accomplishments of the Underground Railroad, few acknowledge the extent to which it relied on Black charitable giving and volunteering for much of its success.

One issue that has been central to discussions of Black self-help is the degree to which the Black community is active in contributing money to help the poor. A greater percentage of Blacks than Whites with incomes of under $12,000 make larger contributions to charitable organizations, similarly, among blacks and whites with incomes between $12,000-$25,000 a higher percentage of Blacks than Whites, with the exception of contributions less than $50, made greater total contributions to charity.

Economics as a Second Language Corporation is a natural extension of the philanthropic propensity that Blacks expressed for themselves and the community of man as a whole. The major difference that we will be putting forward with ESL Incorporated is the utilization of economic principles already at work in society to further the overall goals and objectives of the economic self-sufficiency of our own community, and thereby help the country and the world to prosper.

One area that will not be discussed at any great length in this book is how can Black Americans provide assistance to the continent of Africa in her attempts at building a strong and just continent, while experiencing so much poverty here at home and the answer of course is that before we can help others get their house in order financially we must first have ours in order.

CHAPTER NINE
(THE ROLE OF THE BLACK CHURCH IN COMMUNITY ECONOMIC DEVELOPMENT)

There is no controversy in the fact that the Black Church has been and continues to be the leading institution in the community. The Black Church has no challenger as the cultural womb of the Black community. Not only did it give birth to new institutions such as schools, banks, insurance companies and low income housing, it also provided an academy and an arena for political activities, and it nurtured young talent for musical, dramatic, and artistic development.

Economics as a Second Language Corporation proposes through the use of the ESL Institute to begin the process of coordinating and cataloging the economic development that can be impacted through the Black churches. In a number of communities Black Churches have already taken the lead in developing the economic sensibilities of the community. From the pulpit ministers have for years coordinated the role of the Black community toward the problems that faced the community. They can of course be a powerful force not only in terms of pushing forward the role of ESL Incorporated if we can get them on our side, this can go a long way toward the development of the philosophy that will be successful in encouraging participation in the process.

Emmett D. Carson in his article (Patterns of Giving in Black Churches) states "The Black Churches have provided an essential conduit through which Blacks have traditionally channeled the philanthropic efforts to benefit the less fortunate members of both their own community and the larger society. Noteworthy is the fact that the financial base of many Black churches has eroded as middle class Blacks have moved to the suburbs and formed their own churches. This raises serious questions as to whether or not the Black community should continue to rely upon the Black church as a focal point for funneling their charitable resources to Black organizations."

One way in which the church can continue to lead in this regard is to develop within its hierarchy a department of community economic development with a director of economics, who would oversee the development of the economy of the community surrounding the church. On any given Sunday the parishioners could contribute directly to the fund, which would go toward providing jobs, decent housing, storefront rehabilitation etc.

The fact that the Black church is independent and to a great extent is controlled by the Black community, means that it is perceived as one of the few institutions that has its roots firmly planted within the Black community and the community provides a measure of control over this institution like no other one. Because of early segregation that existed prior to the early 1070's Blacks of all socioeconomic levels found themselves attending a relatively small set of Black churches. These two factors, indigenous control and socioeconomic diversity, made the Black church a unique forum wherein Black people could privately discuss secular and non-secular issues.

When in this book we discuss Black churches, we are discussing them in a non-sectarian fashion, in that we are not talking about one particular church, whether it is Baptist, Catholic, or Protestant, but we are talking about the Black church as a whole. It would be important to begin to overcome some of the barriers that exist in the community between churches of different denominations to have them form associations strictly developed to address the problems of poverty that exist all around them. The concept of Economics as a Second Language would begin hopefully to bring these churches together like never before.

The three major forces in the community will all be brought into the program; the Black Church, the Family, and the youth of the community. We have, therefore, a winning team approach to solving the problems of the community.

Economics as a Second Language attacks the roots of deprivation, which is the lack of information regarding economic development. As has been evident throughout the surge in high technology, information is what the greatest value is in this present age. The information which will be developed and made available to the families through their reunions will be invaluable in terms of alleviating the cycle of poverty and disenfranchisement which is running rampant throughout our community.

Many questions will be raised as to whether or not this approach could be successful; one critical factor in determining the success or failure of this enterprise will be the ability to raise and answer the hard questions concerning this approach to economics. As you read this paper and experience the concepts both original and recycled, my hope is that you make available any questions or comments that you have as to how this program can be instituted.

CHAPTER TEN
(Juneteenth Industries, Inc.), Business Plan

**"Give a man a fish he can feed his family for a day,
Teach a man to fish he can feed his family for a lifetime,
But he must have access to the lake
Ownership guarantees access"**

Anderson Hitchcock

As is clearly stated by the axiom above, it seems that for too long we have been stuck on the notion that, by teaching a man to fish, we have in some way guaranteed his ability to take care of his family. While for a time this might have been the truth. It no longer holds the key to empowering African Americans.

As the caveat, which I added, implies, it is now necessary that we begin to concentrate on ownership of assets as a way of guaranteeing access to the natural resources which allow for the formation of businesses, corporations and foundations, who by there very nature become responsible for providing jobs, cash flow, work force development, capital accumulation and more, for a community of independent individuals.

"Nothing great is ever accomplished without toil and sacrifice". This could be the mantra for the development of the concept to which you are about to be introduced. I have developed Economics as a Second Language (ESL) and Juneteenth Industries, Inc., over the past ten years with a combination of dogged determination and the entrepreneurial zeal of a guru. The mission for the Institute for Economics as a Second Language, Inc. (IESL) has been and remains "The researching and advocating of health, education and economic literacy through family reunions", and the mission of Juneteenth

Industries, Inc. (JTI) is the provision of products and services to the family reunion market.

It has often been said that there are two sides to every issue, but in the case of how to convert the spending power inherent in the family reunion movement in America into a corporation whose dynamism could be unparallel in the history economic theories; we must take into consideration everything that lies between the two sides. Much like the analogy of the two sides of the coin, people often overlook the fact that there also happens to be an edge, where the two sides come together. Where families come together to celebrate their reunions provides the edge upon which great wealth can be built.

This happens also to be true in regards to what can be done with this tremendous potential to build an industry, or should I say to convert what is already an industry into one that has been brought under one corporate umbrella. To this end Juneteenth Industry, Inc. has been born. Together The Institute for Economics as a Second Language, Inc and Juneteenth Industries, Inc. forms both sides of the Family Reunion coin. A non-profit, as well as a private profit making arm. Juneteenth Industries, Inc. is that private profit-making arm.

Our job is to manipulate everything that lies between the two sides, in order to maximize the ability to pool resources and create investment opportunities, which will convert family reunions into a fountain from which will flow economic well being for the entire community.

With the edge given to the African American community by virtue of the popularity of this phenomenon within our community, we definitely have the edge in incorporating this as the sine quo nom, or the axiom around which great wealth can be garnered and redistributed for the betterment of our progeny. We realize that true wealth is that which can be passed down from one generation to the next and built upon.

This is an opportunity through which great wealth can be developed and numerous assets accumulated. In addition this provides a forum and format for the dissemination of economic literacy in a controlled environment, the family reunion. Extensive research conducted by IESL indicates that there are in excess of 1.5 million family reunions that occur every year in the United States and that family members spend between 6 and 7 billion dollars on these events.

Juneteenth Industries, Inc. is being formed as a private profit-making corporation that will provide products and services to the family reunion market. Its mission is to consolidate the travel, tourism and economic development inherent in the family reunion movement into a formidable force for the accumulation of wealth and assets, which will be owned by the primary sponsors of these gatherings, the African American community.

The significance of Juneteenth being used as the corporate name is not coincidental. Juneteenth celebrates the emancipation Proclamation signed by Abraham Lincoln in 1863. However, we know that true emancipation comes only when African Americans control their own economic destiny. Such is the quest of Juneteenth Industries, Inc. in collaboration with its' non-profit arm IESL.

10,000 family corporations will provide direct investment through the purchase of memberships in the Institute for Economics as a Second Language, Inc. These family corporations and their family members will also directly invest through the purchase of shares of stock in Juneteenth Industries, Inc. 9.5 million Shares will be sold by JTI at $10.00 per share. This money will capitalize the construction and operation of nine family reunion resorts throughout the United States, the Caribbean and South Africa.

It is planned that seven family reunion resorts will be built in the United States in or near the following cities: New York, New York, Los Angeles, California, Philadelphia, Pennsylvania, Atlanta, Georgia, San Antonio, Texas, Indianapolis, Indiana and Cleveland, Ohio. In addition, one resort is being planned in Jamaica, West Indies and another in Mtunzini, South Africa. Some areas have already been chosen and architects are busily designing state of the art resorts that will be built on these properties.

In a rural area, about 20 minutes from Cleveland, Ohio, a hundred acre horse farm has been chosen as a back drop for a luxurious resort, which will cater to the needs of families, other associations and groups that want to get away. Families that want to celebrate in a rustic; New England like small town atmosphere will find this resort just the ticket. Chagrin Falls, Ohio sits in the Chagrin Valley and provides for easy access to major theme parks, such as Sea World in Solon, Ohio, or the Rock and Roll Hall of Fame in Cleveland itself.

In the greater Philadelphia, Pennsylvania area, Chester, Pennsylvania has been chosen because of its' central location to much of historic Pennsylvania, from Valley Forge to Independence Hall. Chester provides a focal point around which family reunions will be organized.

A former Museum in Chester, sits on nearly twenty acres in the heart of this once vibrant city, and provides the nucleus around which families have taken their reunions for the past number of years. Negotiations have been entered into to convert this ad hoc family reunion location into a center for the renewal of this city and its' population. It is significant that each location provides not only a perfect opportunity to develop a major tourist destination but beyond that, it promises to relieve critical needs for jobs and redevelopment in communities that have been left behind by the American dream. These resorts will provide decent wages and upward economic mobility for long undeserved population.

Because of the large number of Africans from the Diaspora, who now live in the United States, it is reasonable to consider adding their populations to those who would benefit from this development as well. A resort will be built in Africa as well as one in the Caribbean that will assist in bringing families together for family reunification events.

In Mtunzini, South Africa, talks are underway, for the purchase of a 600-hectare parcel of land, which is located on the Indian Ocean, up the coast from Durban. This is Zulu territory and provides a rich array of cultural and ethnic heritage on display twenty-four hours a day.

The city council of Mtunzini is anxious to provide assistance in the development of this parcel of land for tourism. It is located on an unspoiled sandy beach, which slopes to the Indian Ocean and provides a paradise for adventurous families and their reunions, or for those who want desperately to reconnect with Africa. South Africa is in the grip of redevelopment that offers us a marvelous opportunity to take advantage of a once in a lifetime memory filled event. It also would allow for South Africans who want to visit the United States to reunify with expatriate family members, living in the United States or in the Caribbean.

Not only will these resorts be state of the art, in terms of lodging and dining facilities, but also they will be totally inclusive of spas. Saunas, walking trails, meeting facilities, work out rooms, swimming pools; tennis courts, game rooms, mini theatres and more. Your family will meet in an unmatched atmosphere in which to relax and conduct the financial business of your family corporation.

Some of the products and services that will be provided by Juneteenth Industries, Inc. to the family reunion market will be Family Medical histories, and treatment plans, which will begin to address this problem in future generations. Attorneys, Accountants and financial planners will be on staff, in order to assist families, through their elected representatives, in setting up their family corporations. Financial advisors will consult with families on the better way in which to develop assets and set up education endowments, mutual funds investment trust and more. CD's, Textbooks, workbooks and more, will be available to assist members and their families in debt repair/credit development, asset accumulation. Prepaid financial services will be available along with seminars and workshops on all aspects of financial planning. Burial funds, Land trust, mortgage and deed services will also be provided to members and their families.

As a member of IESL your family will enjoy unlimited access to a family web page which will inform all family members of the progress that is being made to place their family corporation on the best path to economic self sufficiency. Data and family information will be just a keyboard stroke away. All records of the corporation will be available in one location and coordinating reunions will be made streamline and worry free.

Family reunions form fertile ground from which will spring the seeds for the salvation of our communities, our homes and our places of worship. True wealth is defined as an individual who has disposable income, that lives in a community where businesses flourish and entrepreneurship leads to jobs and income, both connected by a place of worship that has sufficient income to allow it to develop the spirit and shape the character of its' residence.

If you would like to assist in this endeavor, we encourage you to become a member of the Institute for Economics as a Second Language, Inc. at the gold level of $250.00, the platinum level at $500.00, or the Diamond level of $900.00. This will entitle you to shares of stock valued at that membership level and any member of you family will then be able to invest through the purchase of shares of stock directly in Juneteenth Industries, Inc. Shares of Juneteenth Industries, Inc. will be sold at ten dollars ($10.00) per share. 95 millions dollars will be raised to accomplish the initial phases of construction and operational completion. Any family unit can purchase up to a maximum of 10, 000 shares.

EXECUTIVE SUMMARY

This Business plan has been developed to present Juneteenth Industries, Inc. to perspective investors and to assist the company in raising 95 million dollars to begin, construction setup and operation of this Family Reunion and wealth creation concept.

I. THE COMPANY

IESL has for the past five years, been involved in the research and surveying of family reunions throughout the world, but most directly in the United States, Jamaica and South Africa. That involvement and the constant development and refinement of the concept of Economics as A Second Language, has lead to the second phase of a three phase, fifteen year plan. This second phase deals with the implementation of a concept, which will lead to the means for economic transformation of the populace and the economic relationships of these three areas of the world directly. The three areas to be most immediately transformed are Mtunzini, South Africa; Mandeville, in Jamaica: and Chagrin Falls, Ohio in the United States. The third phase of the fifteen-year plans deal with the operational and promotional aspects of implementing this plan.

These three areas are distinctly unique from one another, yet amazingly similar in a number of crucial ways. The principal developer and contact for this concept and Corporation is Anderson Hitchcock, who has spent considerable time and money in these three areas developing and researching this investment opportunity. Anderson Hitchcock was born and still resides in Chagrin Falls, Ohio. He has nourished this concept from its humble beginnings in 1987, to its present incarnation. Mr. Hitchcock has developed contacts in the three communities, who wholeheartedly support the work that has been undertaken to bring this concept to its current status.

Before we discuss the uniqueness of these three areas, let's deal with the Countries which each are found and outline the necessity for this undertaking. South Africa has over the past few years, since President Mandela came to power, been searching for a method through which they can bring a majority of the people in the country into the mainstream of economic activity, without upsetting a very precarious balance, namely that segment of the population which currently controls the lions share of the economic pie.

Juneteenth Industries, Inc. deals with the worldwide economic community in a micro and macro economic sense. That sense is how to bring the indigenous population into the existing flow of capital within the countries, as well as, how to create new wealth mechanisms internationally. The sense of how the currency of each country relates in the international marketplace, as well as, within each country.

In Jamaica, we have a different set of concerns, not so much, in brining in a newly arrived constituency, as is the case with the recent elections in South Africa, but a people who have been part of the economy, even though they have not benefited directly from the wealth of the country.

In Jamaica, the necessity is that of creating a much larger pie, one which supplements the effect of all inclusive resorts on the loss of culture and history being available and able to be disseminated to the tourist population. The Jamaica Development Corporation, under the direction of Reverend Garnett Roper will play an essential role in the implementation of this concept throughout the Island of Jamaica.

The last country that will be brought into the equation combines a combination of both influences mentioned above. The Black population in the United States has recently gained political power and is now reaping some of the benefits from that inclusion, but in a larger sense, is just now on the verge of realizing any significant financial benefits from the powerful economic machine that empowers the United States to exercise such major control on the World Economic stage.

The concept of Economics as A Second Language combined with the implementation and control over an embryonic industry; such as that of family reunions could prove to be a major hub around which economic development and entrepreneurship could be spun off. We will get into those later in the business plan.

Juneteenth as a corporate name is significant, because it signifies the Emancipation Proclamation of 1863 signed by Abraham Lincoln, then President of the United States.

Who by proclamation freed those Africans who had been brought to this country purely for the purpose of free labor. Subsequently, this group of individuals were, through Jim Crow and other sinister methods, locked out of the economic spoils during the creation of the American economic infrastructure.

As part of this business plan you will be exposed to the research of the Institute for Economics as a Second Language, Inc. Which was specifically designed to create and implement the collection of data and the statistical analysis to determine the spending power that could potentially be connected with family reunions (See Addendum A)?

Mtunzini is a picturesque town located in Kwazulu Natal on the Indian Ocean in South Africa. It is ideal and has long been known as a place to escape the rigors of more urbanized South Africa. It offers a hospitable work force and will local government, which is prepared to assist on the remaking and selling of this area as a major tourist destination for individuals and families from around the world. Mtunzini has a workforce that is eager to participate in the complete transformation of this community, into one of the most major attractions in the world.

Mandeville, Jamaica is located on the east coast of Jamaica. It is east of Kingston, the capital of Jamaica and a major political and commercial hub. The ongoing concern in Jamaica, by the government and the tourist industry is for a way in which to stabilize and increase the tourist dollar that is being brought to the island.

The government of Jamaica is currently examining proposals to increase the tourist base of the island, and is excited abut the prospect of bringing this family reunion concept to their island. The government would provide the political will to been about the implementation of Economics as a Second Language. The training of certain segments of the population in wealth creation techniques, combined with an increase in tourist arrivals

To the island would receive a great deal of support throughout the Caribbean.

The last community that we will operate in is Chagrin Falls, Ohio, a small town about 25 miles from the heart of Cleveland, Ohio.

Chagrin has a population of nearly 5,000 people the majority of them European in heritage, with approximately one quarter of them of African American Heritage. The significance of this area is that it has a reputation of being a tourist destination for North Eastern Ohio and has the potential with Cleveland gaining prominence as a national and international tourist destination to benefit from the spill over affect. It has a nice quaint atmosphere that can be exploited for its Waterfall and its New England ambiance.

The work forces of these three areas are similar and could be used as a perfect opportunity to discuss the impact from the implementation of Economics as A Second Language as an inherently active component to the implementation of this major economic investment.

II.   Market Potential

Research shows that the Family Reunion Market throughout the world is a growing phenomenon with the potential for developing rapidly into a multi-billion dollar industry. The potential for development of this concept offers the opportunity to change the dynamics of the world economy, and to intimately link the resurgence of the African Continent into a source for the provision of products and services and provide a major impetus to the burgeoning tourism industry worldwide.

This company will approach the marketplace with a combination of sales activity and promotional opportunities. Family Reunion Resorts will be built in all three of these areas simultaneously, and will coordinate and share information and activities on an international level. Each resort will be built around the distinctly unique characteristics inherent to each community. The common element of them all will be there commitment to the Family Reunion and to the concept of Economics as a Second Language.

All aspects of the Family Reunion Industry, as well as, the teaching and implementation of the concept of Economics will be overseen by Juneteenth Industries, Inc. All travel, tours, lodging, entertainment activity at the lodge will be coordinated under one umbrella. In addition, the teaching and dissemination of wealth creation techniques will be handled, with the assistance of legal scholars, financial analysis, investment counselors, credit counselors, and all those experts that will be required to establish family corporations and assisting in the implementation of investment and savings activity.

The Institute will create tailored investment activity for each region in which these lodges are located, and will work with the local government and populace to design approaches to tackling the ingrained patterns of second class citizens that poorer citizens of all countries experience.

A few of the tools of wealth creation will be taught, used and widely disseminated to the populace of these areas are: savings; investment, asset accumulation; entrepreneurship; capital accumulation, home ownership; and job development. These tools will be combined with debt and finance counseling.

The objective is to develop a comprehensive, balance approach to economic development. The Family Reunion business in the United States alone is estimated to encompass approximately 12 million individuals that attend in excess of approximately one million family reunions per year.

It is estimated that over 7 billion dollars is expended by those attending and participating in family reunions. The potential for increasing on a world-wide basis, the number of family reunions occurring yearly, would just about double with the support of the governments of these countries that are being targeted. This support would be channeled toward the launching of a world wide media blitz by the world wide tourist industry.

It is estimated that we could rapidly double the number of families that have reunions. This would give us the extensive network we would need for teaching and coordinating economic activity in these three countries that we have chosen.

With the potential for developing the concept throughout South Africa and Jamaica, the prospect becomes staggering, in terms of its ability to transform the consciousness of many people. The linkages between South Africa, Jamaica, and African Americans, who happen to comprise approximately 70% of the Family Reunion Market, is awesome and portends earth shattering possibilities.

The specific target markets that will be approached most aggressively will be:

- South Africa

- The United States

- The Caribbean

- Europe

- Australia

- Asia

- South America

- Canada

III. Major Milestones

Major Milestones have already been achieved in the effort to bring these regions of the world into a process that could lead to an awakening of economic activity. In July 2000, a presentation was made in Mtunzini to the City Council and to other interested individuals and community leaders, by a group representing Juneteenth Associates.

The property upon which this resort is proposed was toured and the prospects for purchasing the land to be used in this fashion was examined and approved.

This property in Mtunzini offers a vast potential for developing a resort that would rival any, anywhere in the world. The cost of the property is in the area of four million dollars USD. The Kramer farm, as it is known is located in the outskirts of the community and is an excellent site upon which to build this type of resort.

Jamaica has been actively petitioned to take part in the concept as a full participant. The benefits to this region of the world are apparent. Its major focus and economic viability depends upon its ability to attract increased interest in tourism.

Meetings have been held with the Tourism Board and members of the Jamaican Parliament, regarding the feasibility for the implementation of the concept called Economics as a Second Language. The Jamaican Development Corporation is thrilled about the prospect of Family Reunions being attracted to Jamaica and has offered its full assistance.

The process has been approved and the government of Jamaica is looking with great interest to the full implementation of this concept in their country. Full support for the concept has been forthcoming from the private sector as well as from the political and civic segments of the population.

Jamaica offers unsurpassed beauty and a history of accommodating tourist from all over the world. Jamaica is due for resurgence in its number one industry (tourism).

Not only would Family Reunions Lodges, combined with the philosophy of Economics as a Second Language, revitalize the industry in Jamaica, it would give new hope to a region that has had little, in the way of positive news, occur in quite awhile. The purchase price of a beach front parcel of land in Jamaica is estimated at approximately one million dollars USD.

Chagrin Falls, Ohio has a rich and long history of being a tourist destination in North East Ohio, and as a result of the current increase in tourism related activity in Cleveland, Chagrin Falls is becoming a tourist destination with great potential for accommodating the increase in the region. Cleveland has now with the opening of the Rock & Roll Hall of Fame, The Science and Technology Museum; The Jacob's Field complex; and the soon to be open Stadium for the NFL Football team, positioned itself and Northeast Ohio as an international tourist destination.

Chagrin Falls is a 200 year-old community that has a distinctively New England ambiance. The center of attraction is the waterfall and the candy shop that sits right above the waterfall. In addition to its quaint atmosphere, its restaurants, shops, and virtually crime free history provides the perfect scene for family outings and quiet leisurely strolls.

Juneteenth Industries, Inc. is uniquely positioned to take advantage of this opportunity and to bring this most complex plan to fruition. Anderson Hitchcock, the President and founder of Juneteenth Industries, Inc., has for more than a decade, been involved in the research and development of Family Reunions as an industry. In addition he has single handily developed the concept of Economics as a Second Language, which basically states that in order to be a full participant n the economy of a country, one has to be conversant and proficient in the language and concepts of how wealth is created. It is believed and promulgated, by the Institute for Economics as a Second Language, that in order to bring large segments of population into line with economic self-sufficiency the concept of wealth and generational inheritance has to be ingrained in any program attempting to alleviate poverty for a significant portion of the population.

Juneteenth Industries, Inc., and its partners, represents citizens in South Africa, Angola, The United States and Jamaica and Nigeria. It is perceived that this multi-national group of entrepreneurs and business people offer the maximum opportunity to capitalize on the advanced technology now available in the United States and the natural and human resources that are currently coming to the fore in South Africa, Angola, Jamaica, the United States, and Nigeria.

IV. Financial Summary

The plan is to have a four phase release of funds contingent upon certain activity taking place in a time fashion. It is esteemed that the total cost of the three family reunion resorts would be 95 million dollars. The five phases would be undertaken would be:

1. Personnel

2. Planning

3. Construction

4. Operation

5. Marketing/Sales/Advertisement

Business Description

Juneteenth Industries, Inc. is a company the will provide overall project coordination, personnel consideration, construction oversight, marketing, sales and advertisement and operation of these resorts will all be in the hands of Juneteenth Industries, Inc. We estimate and our feasibility study indicates that Family Reunions, early in the twenty first century will be an industry which could generate a billion dollars a year in sales.

In addition to the construction and operation of Family Reunion Lodges and Resorts, Juneteenth Industries, Inc. will be responsible for the implementation of the Economics as a Second Language aspect of the concept. This will involve organizing through churches and the community, the education of individuals, families and organizations win with creation techniques; such as, investment savings, debt counseling, capital accumulation, home ownership, entrepreneurial development, Family Corporations, Educational endowments, budgeting and money management.

All the tools that have been used successfully for years in the more prosperous communities throughout the world will now be taught at family reunions and throughout those communities, by the Institute for Economics as a Second Language.

The Family Reunion Lodges and Resorts will be state of the art facilities, where not only will, individuals and their families are able to congregate for their reunions, but places where individuals will, for a fee, be able to experience an ambiance of total relaxation and rejuvenation.

The lodges will provide suites, dining, facilities, spas, saunas, walking trails, swimming pools, exercise facilities, etc. All of those components will be added, which will make for a memorable experience. Fine dining; entertainment; recreation; tours; wineries, micro-breweries; gift shops; amphitheaters; will be the order of the day for these tourists.

Each facility will have resident accountants; attorneys; financial planners and managers; as well as, consultants of all stripes that will assist these extended family corporations to martial their resources and come away year after year with an increased sense of family property and wealth. Family Corporations, educational endowments; credit unions, seed money for investment activity, a structure around which real wealth will be built and passed on from one generation to the next will be the main focus for these facilities.

Around the family reunion concept, will be built an entire network of financial and commercial activities. Beginning with the travel agencies, limousine and bus services; entertainment activity; professional educators in the culture and history of these regions; caterers, etc. A resort staff, whose only task will be to make every guest, enjoy an unsurpassed and memorable experience at these lodges will trained and employed by Juneteenth Industries, Inc., (JTI)

Combined with these lodges and Resorts will be instituted a world wide celebration of Juneteenth as a national and international holiday. This holiday will sharpen the focus on economic activity on the part of people of color, and will provide concrete opportunities for investment.

Juneteenth, in the United States is already being implemented as the first true African American Holiday. It is the intent of this corporation to attach wealth creation and economic development to this celebration.

It is understood that true freedom, which was alleged with the signing of the Emancipation Proclamation, can only be attained through the creation of an independent sense of wealth and well being which comes from having collateralization.

At these festivities and celebrations, in addition to the dissemination of information on wealth creation strategies, individuals and their families will have opportunities to invest in the lodges and other business ventures, through the Juneteenth Fund which is being implemented strictly as a mutual fund to service this concept and the family reunion industry.

One of the most significant aspects of this program is the need and desire to work with churches, throughout these three countries. We must ingrain in the people the need for economic self sufficiency and get them to endorse this method as a means through which economic stability can be achieved.

The real possibility now exist that an airline, such as, Air Jamaica can be converted to Juneteenth Air, to provide travel services to these various different locations. Also the incorporation of Juneteenth Telecom is underway. A baby bell telephone company is now negotiating to become apart of this concept. This company is African American owned. With the addition of this company the chance increases for real economic development within this framework.

Each resort will be a theme lodge, based upon the history and culture of the location. For instance, in Kwazulu Natal the lodge and facility will be geared toward the tradition and history of the indigenous people of that area and will have a distinctive African legacy.

Visitors to this lodge will be inundated with the culture, history, art, and village life traditionally found in that part of the world. Artisans and Craftspeople, performers, cuisine, will be available to the guests. This will help to create for them a most memorable experience of originality and authenticity.

Jamaica, will likewise, be a resort in which the history, culture, arts and crafts of the indigenous population will be brought to the fore. So that, when guests arrive at this resort it will be anticipated that they will experience the beauty of Jamaica and its people, and not just the warmth of the weather, and the blueness of the ocean. This has recently become the objective of the Jamaican government and the tourist Board in Jamaica. All inclusive resorts have alienated visitors from the people and culture of the island. As a result they miss out on a once in a lifetime opportunity.

Chagrin Falls, in the State of Ohio, has unique opportunity to represent the history of the Underground Railroad, which was used by escaped slaves to make their way to freedom in the North and Canada.

Chagrin Falls is centrally located, in order to be able to visit several locations, which are famous for being stations along the Underground Railroad. Chagrin Falls itself has several homes that were used for such purposes. Not only will these lodges offer relaxation, investment activity, culture and art, but they will also offer a living history of the struggle of an African people to return to its roots and assist in the rebuilding of its continent.

OPERATIONS

The operation of this corporation will be conducted in each region independently with an international offshore corporation overseeing the entire operation. Products and money-making opportunities will be developed from this trademark concept. That of Juneteenth will become recognized worldwide and its products sold worldwide. The three pronged approach will be implemented to provide a maximum opportunity for success. The construction of the lodges will be done simultaneously. All advertisement and marketing will be done jointly from headquarters and regionally. We will us the Family

Reunion as the hub of activity at these resorts but will also market to the general public as well.

The operation of the offshore corporation will be based in Chagrin Falls, Ohio, but it will have offices on the locations as well, and will be connected by email and a 1-800 number, as well as being on the Internet, in order to maximize outreach and customer service. This is an extremely workable new concept, and will herald the dawning of a new age in economic development. The momentum from this will push this concept to the forefront of international attention and give it the impetus it needs to reach the four corners of the earth. At the same time the adjunct concepts of the Juneteenth fund, Juneteenth Telecom and Juneteenth Airlines will be launched. A word about Juneteenth Airlines; Air Jamaica has long been rumored as an airline in trouble, I believe and have every reason to think that the current owner of this troubled airline could be convinced of the correctness of such an opportunity to substantially change the dynamics surrounding this airline, and place it in a position to offer not only passenger service to the continent of Africa, and to increase its services throughout North America, but also to design a cargo operation that could provide transportation for the revitalization of sub-Saharan Africa.

ADVERTISING

Advertising will be done on an international basis, with major publications from travel groups. A major advertising blitz will be launched several months in advance of the opening of these lodges. The blitz will be targeted at major travel associations in Africa, The United States and Jamaica. A heavy emphasis will be placed on publications that cater to the Family Reunion Industry, as well as, to major publications, such as; Ebony, Essence, Jet, Black Enterprise, Emerge. A major campaign will be designed for Black Entertainment Television. In South Africa all opportunities for advertising will be used to reach the populace and to influence their perception of the efficacy of such an undertaking, as this.

It is estimated that a large percentage of the African American population subscribes to at least one of these publications listed above, and that those that do not subscribe, will be exposed to these services, either through the cultural festival, or through massive advertisement in regional publications.

The advertisement will be constructed in such a way that consumers will see not only the opportunity to travel to foreign countries and to experience new cultures, but also to participate and to benefit in a financial sense, as well. The implementation of the concept of ESL will be the guiding principle behind all of our effort.

Consumers will be invited to invest in this concept and to be shareholders in this international Corporation. The advantage of investing in stocks, bonds, mutual funds et al, will be constantly reinforced in all aspects of advertising for the Corporation.

Graphic design firms from the three different regions will be brought together to design a campaign that will be consistent in terms of its approach to selling and implementation for the overall concept. The campaign will be designed to reach selected audiences. All advertising will be overlapping and integrated to maximize coverage and to feed on the coverage being undertaken in each area. Cooperative economics will be a major recurring theme for this promotional activity. A major emphasis will be placed on a telethon of music culture, art that will be held simultaneously in Jamaica, South Africa, and the United States that will be based upon the live aid concerts that have been so successful.

MANAGEMENT AND ORGANIZATION

This section of the business plan for Juneteenth Industries, Inc. outlines the key management personnel, in conjunction with the professional services providers who are assisting with the implementation of the business concept.

I.   OFFICERS

The Company's five principals are:

- Anderson Hitchcock   President

- Merwin Edwards   Finance

- Afonso Eduardo   Secretary

Each of these individuals brings unique capabilities to Juneteenth Industries, Inc.

Anderson Hitchcock has been actively involved in the development of Economics as a Second Language. Over the past two years Anderson has taken the lead, with help from a local foundation in the nationwide surveying of Family Reunions and the tabulation of those survey results.

Over the past few years Anderson has traveled to the three areas intended to benefit from the Family Reunion Lodges. Anderson spent weeks on end traveling throughout South Africa and Jamaica presenting these ideas to the powers that be in those countries hoping to spur interest in a concept which until recently was just an unproven concept. Anderson completed his course work for a Master Degree in Community Economic Development from Case Western Reserve in Cleveland, Ohio. Since then he has dedicated himself to implementing the concept of Economics as a Second Language.

Merwin Edwards has an undergraduate degree from Hampton University in Virginia, and has been actively involved as an investor and a strategist in bringing this concept to this current state. Merwin has committed unlimited time and energy to the concept of ESL and is poised with his computer knowledge to aid in setting up a worldwide computer network that will be used to coordinate activity in these areas.

Afonso Eduardo is an Angolan National, and has been invaluable in helping to determine the way that this concept would look and how important it is for a concept such as this to be in effect, in order to give residents of these and other countries hope that there is a way in which their economic malaise can be lifted and they will be able to enter into the mainstream of economic development that has eluded them thus far.

Afonso Eduardo was for a number of years, the head of the American Desk for the Angolan Government in Luanda, Angola. I first met Afonso in 1997 while on a fact- finding mission to the country of Angola. At that time after length discussions with Afonso he came on board as a member of the team working to design and implements this concept.

ADVISORY GROUP

In addition to the above mentioned individuals, Juneteenth Associates is pleased to have a group of advisors, who will act to ensure that all major elements are in place, in order to guarantee a business which operates at its highest rate of efficiency. There are three individuals that act as unpaid consultants for Juneteenth Associates. They do this out of friendship to Anderson Hitchcock, and because of the fact that they have expertise that can be helpful to the overall success of this enterprise.

Mr. Daniel Berry, formerly the Associate Director of the George Gund Foundation was responsible for providing funding to assist in the collection of data regarding family reunions. He is now the Vice President for Labor force development at the Greater Cleveland Growth Association. The Growth Association acts as the Chamber of Commerce and Business Development for major Corporations throughout Northeast Ohio.

Mr. Berry has been intimately familiar with the work of the Institute for Economics as a Second Language, and has been instrumental in consolidating the philosophy and concepts inherent in ESL. He has for the past ten years been unofficial advisor to Mr. Anderson Hitchcock on the development of this concept.

Mr. Charles Burkett is the Minority Economic Development Specialist for the Enterprise Development Corporation. EDI is teamed up with Case Western Reserve University's Weather head School of Management which trains managers through their MBA program to perform at high rates of efficiency in the corporate world. EDI acts as an incubator and provides overall business acumen to entrepreneurs for start up or expansion of business throughout the city of Cleveland and all of Northeastern Ohio. They will provide an invaluable service to the development and implementation of this concept.

The third person that forms the Advisory Group for Juneteenth Associates is Mr. Kevin Jones. Mr. Jones is the President of his own minority venture capital firm, and also leads Obsidian Investments Inc. a membership investment mutual fund that recently was charted to assist with business development in the African American community.

Mr. Jones is also the Vice President for the Northeast Fund. Minority Venture Capital Firm, which provides funds to leverage private funds that can be used to shore up under capitalized enterprises throughout the African American community. These nine individuals have devoted considerable time and energy to getting this business up and operating and will continue to provide the oversight necessary to guarantee a profitable business experience. Juneteenth Associates presents a credible group of principles, with professional support and advisors.

PRODUCTION SCHEDULE

The schedule for the implementation of this concept was broken down into three five year phases. The first phase was that of gathering information and data which could be used to determine the prospect for success of such a venture. That phase was carried out between 1993 and 1998.

The second phase is the one we are entering now, and that is the Construction phase for the Family Reunion Resorts themselves.

This phase is approximately five years in length and should be accomplished by the year 2003.

The final phase is one of advertising, marketing and operations. The third and final phase which should lead to the full operation of these resorts is scheduled to last from 2003 through 2008.

SALES

It is estimated that sales of family reunions and individual vacation slots could number into the thousands by the time of the scheduled opening of the resorts. Initially hundreds of gatherings should be booked for the first year of operation. With each Family Reunion averaging hundreds of individuals it is conceivable one million people to could use these facilities in their first year operation.

FINANCIAL COMMITMENTS

It is estimated that financial commitments totaling approximately 95 million dollars will be required. It is hoped that this will derived with the assistance of the World Trade Organization and private investors in 1998. We are currently operating on an initial investment of $100,000 from Dr. Mbanefo.

ADVERTISEMENT/MARKETING/SALES

It is estimated that the first advertising for these resorts will begin to appear in the year 2002. Reservations will be taken by a worldwide system that will be developed and up and operating early in the year 2002. We will note in our early advertisement that the need for individuals to secure dates early will be critical to ensure availability in one of these three facilities.

STRUCTURE AND CAPTALIZATION

Juneteenth Associates began doing business in 1998 and the States of Ohio. It is anticipated that Juneteenth Associates will be totally capitalized with the injection of 95 million dollars. In addition, funds will be raised by the selling of share of stock in different subsidiaries of the Corporation and in the Family Reunion Resorts themselves.

EXECUTIVE SUMMARY

As an elemental, but critical factor in developing a comprehensive marketing plan, I will begin this paper with the quote "Marketing is the art of building demand for ones product." As is also the case when looking at selling a product, it is first necessary to educate the consumer as to the nature of the problem, and then to introduce them to the solution which is contained within your product.

The organization which I will use to demonstrate my marketing plan is the Institute for Economics as a Second Language or simply the Institute. The Institute is a non profit organization, incorporated under Federal Government regulations 501 ©3 of the Internal Revenue Code for Tax Exempt Organizations.

The Institute is a research and training organization responsible for the design and implementation of innovative economic development strategies and learning approaches. As a service, the institute provides lifelong opportunities in the principles of economic understanding and development, along with planning for individuals from grades kindergarten through adulthood.

The mission of this non profit organization is to improve the public's literacy, comprehension and direct application of those economic development principles in ways that ultimately translate into asset development, financial stability and growth. To empower individuals, families and communities to coalesce around fundamental issues of economic survival, through a host of self evaluation, resource sharing, planning and implementation activities, is the goal to which IESL and Juneteenth Industries, aspire.

Economics as a Second Language is a transformative philosophy predicated on the belief that; regardless of national origin or language, one must first become literate in the basic principles of economics as a means of gaining full participation and mobility within the society.

The institute is a Chester, Pennsylvania based organization founded in 1995 in Cleveland, Ohio. The Corporation was formed to promote economic parity among African Americans and other people of color, who are currently excluded from mainstream economic participation. Anderson Hitchcock, a community economic developer, is the founder and incorporator of this organization.

The institute grew out of the work of the Juneteenth Society for Historic and Economic Development; a California based organization that examined the economic relationships within the Black community of San Jose, California and observed the growing trend of families coming back together around extended family; linear concepts of the Black Family Reunion. The two major institutions within the Black community are the family and the Black church. Therefore, it can be reasonably assumed that if the accumulation of wealth is to be accomplished it would have to be around these two institutions.

In the early 1980's, this observation led to expounding the theory of Economics as a Second Language, which recognizes that regardless of your primary language or position within society, one cannot be successful within America's free enterprise – capital intensive structure, without being conversant in the language of economics; while at the same time able to conceptualize and institutionalize wealth being gathered by the extended family as a whole.

Dr. Michael Sherraden states, in his book Assets of the Poor, "Wealth is not income, spending, and consumption, but rather savings, investment and accumulation of Assets." The job of any economic development strategy then becomes how we develop an instrument (institution) within the Black community to do just that.

The institute would be just such an instrument. The institute would provide the training, organizing, and resources to begin to disseminate this understanding, using family reunions and church based economic entities as the hubs around which this movement could be based. Since 1989 elements of the ESL working group have been meeting and exploring various methods of organizing the necessary resources, both material and human, that would allow for a comprehensive approach to addressing this vacuum that exist within the Black community, on how to bring about slow, methodical evaluation, with recommendations as to how to proceed from there.

It is estimated by the members of the working group that it will take a minimum of three to five years before the institute would be at a point where it could begin to provide the products and services; such as workbooks, curriculum, lesson plans, audio and videotapes, as well as consultants in various program areas, like investments, dividends, tax breaks for family corporations providing seminars to members on all aspects of asset development and capital formation. If nothing is done to begin to deal with the economic education and development within the Black community, the level of economic determinism will continue to be the great bane that it has proven to be in the past. This method offers a viable alternative to the continued dependents on governmental programs, which foster dependence on others, while those that are most directly affected by the inability to form pools of capital are condemned to a status of second class citizenship.

COMPETITION

Because of the fact that we are the developers of this product line, we will be competition free in the initial stages. Even though on a much broader scale we will be in competition with general individual economic development or more specifically profit making businesses who promise through seminars, a method of getting rich quick; the differences are sufficient enough that it is estimated that no serious competition for the product now exist or will exist for the foreseeable future.

GOALS

Major goals of the institute will be as follow:

1. To within the first year of the organization have developed and put into place down through the second level of the distribution network. (See attached schematic)

2. Within the second year add level three to the distribution network.

3. Within the third year add level four and begin distribution at the end of the year.

4. Within that same three year period, identify and reach at least thirty percent of the eligible customers through various techniques such as personal selling and mass media.

5. Develop a database of current family reunions and identify ten churches within each state level for targeting these products.

STRENGTHS AND WEAKNESSES

STRENGTHS

1. The rapid growth of family reunions in the Black community. It is estimated that sixty percent of black people currently attend yearly family gatherings and the trend is for more growth over the next ten years.

2. The Black Church has long been one of the wealthiest institutions in the Black community and leads in the understanding the need for economic self-sufficiency on the part of the community.

3. As the poorest segment of the American populace it is a community that is ripe for economic development philosophies.

4. It is estimated by some leading economist that the wealth of the Black community in America if taken as a whole would make this population the ninth largest economic block in the world. This makes the Black community a significant potential market for these products.

WEAKNESSES

1. Development of a program this extensive has certain built in risk because of the shear weight of the institution that has to be brought together.

2. The concept of extended families being used as a medium for economic development is completely new and potentially revolutionary in impact.

3. The amount of research done on this concept has been negligible.

4. It will be necessary to overcome some natural inhibitions about who to trust with your money. Whether this be personal or institutional mistrust.

POSITIONING THE PRODUCT

Primary segmentation would be along the following lines: the Black family reunions, geographic segmentation, major Black churches and major Black universities. Audio and video tapes would be marketed to schools, individuals, churches and libraries and most significantly to family reunions through the use of seminars, workshops and the media. A toll free 800 number would be established for ordering the product. A separate marketing mix would be developed for each specific target market. The marketing mix would determine what are the most significant selling points for the products and services provided by JTI. Will it be the product, price or the distribution that will be highlighted as the selling mechanism? Or will it be a combination of all of the above.

PROMOTIONAL ACTIVITIES

All four of the customary forms of promotion will be enlisted to sell these products. Oral communication on a person to person basis, or personal selling could perhaps be the critical element in the promotional activity of these products, because of the fact that if you are able to penetrate even a few family reunions, it is a good bet that you will have individuals from throughout the country, who upon their return home would be a major promotional element.

Advertising could be effective, because of the ability to segment certain audiences for the product there is a number of Black publications that could be targeted as well as a significant number of radio stations that cater to the Black community and some national television stations that could be targeted. Fourthly, sales promotions which offer discounts for becoming a member of the institute could produce some very favorable promotional activities. In addition, aggressive marketing at the fourth level of the marketing distribution network, which is down to the level of the cities, could produce some rewards.

PRODUCT

The product that this marketing plan will focus on is the educational products that will be offered to our customers. Educational products will be of three different formats; curriculum, video and audio tapes and training manuals.

OBJECTIVES

The major objectives of the institute are as follow:

1. To position the institute in the forefront of Black community economic development.

2. To produce a quality educational product.

3. To begin to pool the economic resources of the Black community.

4. To strengthen economic family values.

5. To create an institution in the Black community dedicated to the proposition of economic self-sufficiency for Black people.

6. To end the cycle of poverty and illiteracy inherent in the Black community.

7. To create an infrastructure within the Black community that is dedicated to the creation of assets and capital pools, which can be used to educate and provide for future generations of Black people in America.

Because of the impact that this institute could have on reversing the poverty in urban and minority communities it is likely to assume that the media would pick up on the social implications of what we are doing, and that they would be interested in featuring different elements of the organization in news stories that could reach millions of individuals free of charge.

The Marketing Director on the national level would be responsible for the development of the organizational marketing network throughout the country, with the Associate Director responsible for product development. The secretary would provide support for the Director and the Associate Director. Consultants would be hired to work in the following areas:

1. Curriculum Development

2. Audio and Video Tapes

3. Management Information Systems

4. Training Manual Development

A monitoring system would be put into place to make sure that the organizational structure as well as product development proceeds along realistic, achievable schedules from start to completion of product and distribution of same.

CHAPTER ELEVEN
(Black Family Reunion Registry)

In order for the program of IESL to be successful, we must put together a listing of those families that are already engaged in family reunions and begin the process of cross matching individuals accordingly. As families come together to start reunions of their own, IESL would be there to provide them with invaluable information as to how to proceed with the development of their family corporations and foundations right from the beginning so that valuable time and energy will not be wasted but will not be wasted but will be utilized to the advantage of the family members and the communities that they represent.

The BFRR would be a national database of linear and extended family member reunions. For instance, The Hitchcock Family Reunion and up to five contact people would also be listed. The Hitchcock family, in order to be listed in the registry, would pay a nominal fee that would entitle them to information from IESL Inc in regard to areas of interest and to a publication or newsletter that would be used to inform family reunions of trends that are taking place in the family reunion movement. And let us make no mistake; it is just that, a movement who's potential to reshape the relationship of the black community to the rest of America could indeed be phenomenal.

The family reunions would be listed in five different categories that would be based upon the region in which the family would be based, that would be the central location or the hub location around which every family reunion is based. In regard to The Hitchcock Family Reunion, it would be the South region because every other year the family reunion is held in Athens, Georgia, which is the area where the majority of the family settled following the emancipation proclamation. The other regions which would be listed would be the Northeastern region of the country, the Mid America region, the Western region, the Caribbean region. The BFRR would become the cornerstone upon which IESL Inc. would be built. It is estimated that there are in existence today, upwards of 1.5 million black family reunions that are now taking place throughout America. These reunions have not been cataloged and have yet to be viewed in the proper perspective as to what potential they hold for rerouting the restoration of the black community. The myriad of problems that the black community faces on a daily basis, can only be addressed as the monolith that it is and to attempt to provide band-aid solutions when the community is hemorrhaging means that the problems will not only continue but will increase in severity. We must take into consideration what this means not only to the black community, but this could be transferred to its effect upon the whole of the fabric of American Society.

This is a movement that is waiting to be coordinated towards some sort of positive end. It is like a fruit that is ready for the picking. We cannot allow it to rot on the vine; but must seize the time and bring it into some coordinated force that can have a positive effect throughout the country. IESL proposes to do just that.

The method, through which this would be brought about, would require a concerted massive public relations campaign which could begin to reach the families that are already involved in reunions and to spur the creation of new family centers. It is easily envisioned that the majority of Black Americans prior to the turn of the century could be attending a family reunion.

A public relations campaign, unlike any that has ever been launched before, would have to be undertaken and targeted specifically to the African American community. All national publications such as Jet, Ebony and Essence magazines would be solicited to run advertisements describing this undertaking. All major Black newspapers such as The Call and Post and others of a regional nature would be contacted and ads would be taken out in them. Membership forms would be included upon which the information would begin to be gathered would and flow into this national database. National Black Networks and Radio stations would be contacted to run advertisements and public service announcements that would underscore the need to sign up and get your family through the use of Cable Television. The NAACP through its regional and national network could be enlisted to provide assistance in this endeavor.

One thing that is abundantly clear is that the public relations campaign would have to be well though out and possibly an agency would be brought on board as a consultant to make sure that all possible methods of disseminating this information would be explored. The confidentiality of this information would have to be guaranteed, because if it were to fall into the wrong hands, it cold conceivably is used for negative purposes. Recognition has not been forthcoming for the energy that has gone into the planning and elevation of this form of family development to the height tat it currently enjoys today. The BFRR would allow for the highlighting of the individuals and families that are moving these reunions to new vistas within the conscience of the black community.

The impact that family reunions have had upon the psychology of the black community has yet to be measure. But we can be assured that it has been great and will continue to play a major role in bringing the extended black family back together in a way that nothing heretofore has been able to do. I believe, however, that in order for the black community to reach its full potential through family reunions it is necessary that the family reunion concept be institutionalized and the rigors of organizational behavior be utilized to determine the most efficient routes for arriving at a clear and concise perspective on how to make the most of these reunions.

Over the course of approximately the past two decades, family reunions have grown at a phenomenal rate. Prior to the 1970's, it was rare to hear of a family reunion taking place even though there were a few, the vast majority of family reunions have only been organized within the past ten years. Every year more black families are coming together for the first time across all lines; geographic, class, and educational, to reestablish, or in some cases, to establish ties that had been broken as long ago as the end of the civil war.

IESL is currently establishing a data base of 6,000 family reunion use surveys that have been filled out from all throughout the United States. It is the hope that 10,000 families will form the core for the implementation of this concept, simply by filling out the survey and then becoming members of the Institute for Economics as a Second Language, Inc.

Through this registry, families will more easily be able to coordinate family related activity, whether it is their reunion, a side trip to some remote destination, or utilizing the benefits of their burial fund, wedding fund, or in the event that sufficient demand is there, perhaps a health plan implemented through their family corporation for family members.

The possibilities go so far, that all of the benefits that would accrue from having this registry, cataloged and chronicled for easy access have not even been considered. It will be up to each family corporation to determine how best to use their corporations.

Each family corporation will have access to its own web site and be connected to family members from around the world. It will be a wonderful way in which family members will be able to stay in contact with one another regardless of how often they move. They will always have a way of maintaining contact with one another.

CHAPTER TWELVE
(Family Reunion Use Survey)

It is incumbent upon our community to fill this survey out and get it back to IESL, so that your family can be included in the growth and development of this exciting new imitative.

INSTITUTE FOR ECONOMICS AS A SECOND LANGUAGE, INC.

3502 W. Slauson Ave

Los Angeles, California 90043

323-898-3064

Institute4esl@juno.com

www.IESL.com

"Researching and Advocating Health, Education and Economic Literacy through Family Reunions"

_____

Name of person filling out survey

_____

Address

_____

City/State   Zip Code

_____

Area Code   Telephone Number

E-mail address_____

FAMILY REUNION HISTORY

1. Does your family host a reunion?   Yes____   No____

   If yes, are you a contact person for your family's reunion? Yes____ No____

If no, please provide us with the name and number of someone we can contact for more information about your family reunions.

(Maternal Reunion)   **(Paternal Reunion)**

_____   _____

Name of contact person   Name of contact person

_____   _____

Address   Address

_____   _____

City/State   Zip Code   City/State   Zip Code

_____   _____

Area Code   Telephone #   Area Code   Telephone #

2. How are often are your family reunions held? _____

3. How long has your family held a reunion?

   0-10 years_____   11-19 years_____   20+ years_____

4. How many people generally attend your family reunions?

   0-100_____   101-249_____   250-500_____   500 & above_____

5. Name the last three cities in which your family hosted a reunion?

_____

6. What names are your family reunions held under?

_____

7. When you travel to a family reunion, how do you travel?

   Bus____ Car____ Plane____ Train____Other (specify)_____

8. While at your family reunion, where do you generally stay?

   Hotel____ Motel____ With relatives____ Other (specify)_____

9. While at your family reunion, where do you typically eat?

   Restaurant____Catered event____ Relatives' house____
   Other (specify)_____

10. While at your family reunion, what types of activities are or would you like to see provided?

____Dance	____Family Showcase	____Tours
____Award dinners	____Facials	____Family Seminars
____Workshops	____Beautician Services	____Investment Seminars
____Family Trees	____Barber Services	____Video Taping
____Exercise classes	____Church Services	____Dry Cleaning
____Full Service Spa/Sauna	____Grave Site Visits	____Child Care
____Swimming	____Youth Activities	____Other (specify)_____

11. Would you support a family reunion resort in an urban area near you?

    Yes____ No____

12. Would technical assistance be helpful in planning your family reunion?

    Yes___ No____

13. What family reunion memorabilia do you now purchase, or would you like to purchase while at your Family reunion?

_____Tee Shirts   _____Key Chains

_____Caps   _____Sweat suits

_____Mugs   _____Family crest

_____Other (specify)_____

14. How much money would you estimate that you spend on the following events associated with your family reunion?

_____Travel   _____Tours

_____Lodging   _____Entertainment

_____Food   _____Memorabilia

_____Drink   _____Shopping

_____Other (specify)_____

15. How would you rate your investment expertise?

____Very Good   ____Good   ____Average

____Poor   ____Very Poor

16. Does your family have a family corporation or family business?

Yes____   No____

17. Does your family have an educational endowment established?

Yes____   No____

18. Would you like to see your family start an educational endowment?

Yes____   No____

19. Please identify your place of worship. Be as specific as possible. If none, please write "none."

Name_____

Address_____

City/State/Zip Code_____

Pastor/Leader_____

Area Code/Telephone Number_____

20. Do you own your own company?   Yes____   No____

21. Do you or does someone in your family own farmland? If so, in what State_____

22. What is your company Name? _____

_____

Address?_____

State _____Zip Code _____

Phone #_____

23. What is your company e-mail address?_____

COMMENTS:_____

_____

_____

_____

_____

Thank you for assisting us with this research project. The information will help to design economic development strategies to utilize the church and family reunions as centers of wealth creation in our communities.

All information gathered in this survey is kept strictly confidential and is used only for the purposes for which it is gathered. No list of names will be sold to marketing firms or anyone else.

CHAPTER THIRTEEN
(Ghenmor Import/Export Trading Co, Inc.)

As the natural extension of the concept of ESL international trade and development between African from the Diaspora, whether they be found in the United States, the Caribbean or on the continent of Africa makes perfect sense. One of the overwhelming realities is that in order for African American to overcome centuries of inadequate economic development, we must begin to look to the natural resources still available in Africa.

The question then becomes how are we to implement and international trade regime, which can not only create jobs on both side of the equation, but also how we can use international trade and development to benefit inner city communities. As we transport people between family reunion resorts are there not opportunities to transport cargo and supplies as well. I believe that there is and as a result of this believes I have been pursuing accreditation through Temple University in International trade and development.

Armed with a certificate from Temple, and knowledge of the industry it began to make perfect sense to connect a network between the Caribbean, Africa and the United States. What you then have is two of the most powerful industries coming together to form a basis for real and sustained economic growth in the African American community. One of the unique aspects of this concept is that everyone benefits on all sides of the equation. We are able to obtain raw, natural resources from Africa, and export products both to the Caribbean and to Africa.

Mutuality of exchange of Tourism and Cargo enables the formation of a multi faceted relationship that encourages not only self sufficiency, but exposes people to opportunities here to fore impossible. International trade and investment opens up a broader venture for the success of this concept. Because of the fact that we are building a resort both in the Caribbean and in South Africa provides a platform for launching this venture with a higher probability of success than normal.

Ghenmor Import/Export Trading Co. was formed in the year 2000 with a mission of providing goods and services worldwide in a timely and efficient manner. In many of the communities where the family reunion resorts are being built there happens to be a thriving port or harbor. For Instance, Chester, Pennsylvania has unlimited access to the harbor for commercial trade vessels. Los Angeles, Atlanta, and New York all provide open access to international trade and development.

The two largest employers in the world are tourism and international trade and development. It is incumbent upon us then to design ways in which these two powerful industries can be brought together around the concept of asset accumulation and capital formation.

Families who become a part of IESL will have opportunities to invest in both of these industries in a way that has never before been conceived of, and if it has been thought of up until now there was no practical way to make this happen.

As we come together and pool our resources around family reunions, some of those funds need to be used to spur international trade and development. This also gives our community an opportunity to begin to establish African Americas as a force for addressing the intractable problems that face our brethren throughout the third world.

Have you ever looked at pictures of starving children in Africa and wondered why is there nothing that I as an African American can do to help this part of the world. While others a focused on solving problems in other parts of the world, Africa is continually neglected, because those descendants of Africa that have the most in common with the continent find themselves unable to control their own economic futures let alone someone's economic future in Zimbabwe or Tanzania.

I refer back to Mr. Erbie Phillips, when he states in "Winning the Economic Development Championship" that when any group does not produce goods and services they must "trade" to obtain them, and this can lead to a situation known as a "trade imbalance" Black owned business receipts are approximately 10% of what black consumers spend annually on goods and services, therefore, blacks export 90% of their income.

According to Mr. Phillips, it may be necessary or more efficient for one group to manufacture certain goods or products, while importing different goods or services from other groups. This exchange is known as "trade". Whether we like it or not it is currently necessary for blacks to purchase most of their goods and services from people other than blacks. As consumers begin to understand "terms of trade" we will be able to participate in the process of obtaining lucrative benefits, in the form of reinvestment, from businesses which target the black consumer market.

Ghenmor Import/Export Trading Co. is designed to begin to address this imbalance. Ghenmor Import/Export Trading Co. is located in the city of Chester, Pennsylvania in a federal hub zone. It has an advisory committee of 10 individuals who have long been involved in the field of international trade. It has contact throughout the Delaware River Port Authority, the Department of Commerce, and The Department of Agriculture and is listed as a minority owned company.

Ghenmor Import/Export Trading Co. was founded by Anderson Hitchcock, Merwin Edwards and Afonso Eduardo to be used as just such a vehicle to enter the international trade market on behalf of African American through the utilization of funding being invested through the family reunion concept. As families come under the umbrella of IESL they will be afforded access to information on how they might capitalize from their investment through international trade and development.

Is there a precedent for groups of individuals thinking that through the use of international trade and development a sound economic footing could be implemented? I don't think that we have to look very far to see that indeed there is. For example:

- o The United States became an economic super power because of its ability to manufacture and export aerospace and defense goods to other countries.

- o Japan's economy soared to all time highs because of their ability to manufacture and export automobiles. Robotics and electronics.

- o During the 1990's. Other Asian countries, especially China, will continue to experience above average economic growth because of their ability to efficiently manufacture an array of electronic products, computers, and household appliances.

Let see if we as a people cannot define a relationship to the natural resources currently possessed in different African countries to manufacture some products that can then be returned as consumer goods. In this manner everyone benefits from increased trade and development.

I once heard a young women complaining vehemently about the fact that all synthetic hair purchased in the black community is being sold by non black people. People who don't even use the product, but recognizer others dependence upon it. Why are we not able to produce synthetic hair somewhere in our community and provide jobs for our own people?

African Americans have long been labeled as "good consumers" The assumption is that "If you have a product, black people will buy it." Many embers in the community acknowledge this as a statement of truth. They view this as a negative characterization, especially when considering the lack of direct investment made by black people into community owned business ventures.

However, until the day comes when black people are investing in their communities we need to establish new "terms of trade". The new terms should be that, "if businesses want to obtain our loyal patronage, then they must reinvest some of their profit back into the communities from which they can it.

I will discuss later in this book how I believe we can use this concept to have a tremendous impact on what we do as a community to transform raw materials coming from Africa into goods and services that can begin to address century's old problems of inadequate cash flow and business development. I must say that not much is going to change in our communities unless and until, both the church and the family reunion can be brought into an agreement which realizes and admits the problems and addresses squarely the need for some solutions.

To this end IESL is dedicated, and with the assistance of individuals like you who read this book and decide that it is long past time to take a risk on behalf of future generations, we will reach our goals and objectives.

We will provide for those who deserve to have a generation or two of sound financial planning behind their efforts to impact their families, their communities and their churches, a respite from the numbing effects of poverty and provide them with inspiration to achieve financial security, beyond the wildest dreams of those who came before, namely our ancestors who landed on these shores so many centuries ago.

CHAPTER FOURTEEN
(The Wealth Network)

The Wealth Network is the concept that in my mind pulls all of the divergent aspect of the family reunion concept together. Because of the gigantic nature of the undertaking, it has been necessary for me to develop each element independently, while at the same time making sure that there is coherence, and a consistency in my train of thought.

For that the powers that be gave me the concept of a network of wealth that would allow for family corporations to diversify their investments while contributing to a thoroughly flushed out system of wealth creation. That system comes in the form of THE WEALTH NETWORK.

Can you imagine a concept that has at its roots a philosophy that not only empowers people to conceive and achieve wealth in a new way, but one in which both non profits and private profit making corporations have equal validity and equal wait. Some might ask what are the major and inherent differences in what the two types of organizations can do, and where does one start and the other leave off.

This is a dilemma with which I have wrestled from the beginning of my efforts to bring ESL together. It was not until recently that the idea can to me that what is really being established through ESL is a network of companies that form a platform to provide our community with the best possible chance of reversing centuries of inactivity.

The primary difference between a non profit organization and a private profit making one is what can be done with the profits that are made by each. Just because an organization is incorporated as a not for profit organization, does not mean that it cannot make profit. On the contrary, it is inherent on organizations to produce profit for its survivability.

The phrase that sums up the differences, is that for a not for profit corporation, the profits "cannot inure to the benefit of one individual, but must be returned to the organization to further the purpose for which the organization was formed". This is why I recommend that the family corporation be formed as a not for profit organization. I also recommend that every family corporation has a for profit arm. We will discuss this more in subsequent chapters.

The Wealth Network is comprised of several corporations. Let me outline them for you here, so that you might have a better understanding of the magnitude of the undertaking which is ESL. The first organization formed as a part of this concept was IESL, the Institute for Economics as a Second Language, Inc. Without going into much discussion of this organization now, suffice it to say that this organization has developed the philosophical underpinnings of ESL, Economics as a Second Language.

IESL, Inc is a not for profit organization. What this means is that under Federal and State Law contributions to this organization may be deducted as charitable contributions by patrons, who chose to support the work of IESL. Under 501©3 provision of the law, both Federal and State, IESL is not only Tax exempt, which means that the organization does not have to pay State of Federal Taxes, but it is also Tax Deductible, which means that all, or a portion of the contributions made by the public can be deuced from the Federal taxes and State Taxes. Much like contributions made to your Church, Synagogue or Mosque.

Non profit sector of the economy operates to provide services and is some cases products that either the government or the private sector have overlooked, or decided that there is not sufficient profit to stimulate much interest. On the other hand the non profit sector believes that these services are essential to living a comfortable life style for the public. It might also be that the services or products provided by not for profits allow for altruistic minded patrons to support causes that might otherwise go under funded, or not be provided at all because of the narrow profit margin.

On the other hand private profit making corporations generally are limited in terms of what they can do with their profits only by the type of corporation that is set up by the owners or share holders of the corporation. For profit corporations, have a totally different tax structure from not for profits.

Without going into detail to much in this book, I will only discuss a few types of for profit corporations. The major ones are C Corporations, S Corporations, Limited Liability Corporations, or Sole proprietorships. These corporations speak primary to three issues, those issues are ownership, tax liability or fiduciary responsibility.

In addition to IESL, the not for profit member of The Wealth Network, you have Juneteenth Industries, Inc., which provides products and services to the family reunion industry. You also have Ghenmor Import/Export Trading Co. Inc. whose mission the provision products and services through international trade and development, primarily between the Caribbean, the United States and Africa.

Along with those three members of The Wealth Network you also have Seven Days of Kwanzaa.Com, a company designed to take advantage of the Kwanzaa holiday in terms of the provision of products and services to this rapidly expanding market. Finally, you have RoughGemauction.Com, an online service for the importation of precious and precious stones for use as a source of job and economic development in the African American community.

Each of these companies will be touched on a little later in this book. But suffice it to say that The Wealth Network is a well though out system of commerce that has the potential to provide a flow of capital into our community unlike any that has ever been seen before. The closes thing that my research has revealed to what is being envisioned here is the Black Star Line as proposed by the

Honorable Marcus Garvey. This concept takes some of his ideas and brings them into the twenty first century.

The major departure from his philosophy is the utilization of the family reunion, which has grown exponential of the past few decades in terms of its potential to be a nucleus and a catalyst for the fulfillment of his dreams and aspirations.

As other companies are envisioned and researched that can add impetus to the quest for capital development and asset accumulation in the African American community they will be added to The Wealth Network and will assist in meeting the requirements for capital to develop and implement this radical system of self empowerment.

I hope that this helps you as a potential participant in the success of this concept to understand how and why all of these corporations were developed, and to gain new insight into how through working together to establish this Wealth Network we are taking a gigantic leap forward in terms of reaching our long term economic and financial goals and objectives.

CHAPTER FIFTEEN
(The Institute for Economics as a Second Language, Inc.)

The Institute for Economics as a Second Language, Inc. (IESL), is a 501(c) 3 not for Profit organization, which has for the past seven year's extensively researched issues And investment strategies combining the economic spending power of religious institutions working closely in conjunction with the Family Reunion Movement in America. The creation of investment strategies utilizing a combination of Religious, Community and Family resources would form the core of a new effort to revitalize inner city America.

Anderson Hitchcock, MA, founded the IESL, Inc. in Cleveland, Ohio in 1995, with a grant from the George Gund Foundation. The original focus of the organization was to determine the nature, scope and importance of family reunions in the African America community. A Family Reunion Use survey was developed and 2500 surveys were conducted in communities across the country during 1995 and 1996. Cities which were surveyed were Philadelphia, Pennsylvania; Cleveland, Ohio; Washington, D.C.; Atlanta, Georgia; San Antonio, Texas; Los Angeles, California and Indianapolis, Indiana.

In 2002, Mr. Anderson brought IESL to Pennsylvania; formed a multi-cultural Advisory Committee and revised and updated the Family Reunion Use Survey. The three page survey, poses questions regarding the frequency; number of family members in attendance; mode of travel and lodging; costs incurred; preferred activities and level of investment expertise.

During August and September 2002, 1,000 surveys were conducted in the Philadelphia, P A and Los Angeles, CA areas. Based on the data gathered in these surveys and those conducted in 1995/96, it is estimated that approximately one million African American family reunions are held in the United States each year. It is also estimated that between six and seven billion dollars is spent yearly on these gatherings. Some of the reunions have as few as ten people in attendance; while others range in the hundreds.

Through the family reunion surveys, IESL has obtained the first definitive study of the history and extensive nature of African American family reunions in America; the spending power of participants and the potential for using reunions as a means of education and empowerment. IESL has positioned itself as a repository of data on how individuals spend their money when it comes to family reunions.

In terms of populations served, family reunions include a broad spectrum of society. While it is true that to this point, most family reunions (estimated to be between 70 and 80%) have been organized and carried out in the African American community, it is reasonable to assume that this concept would be appealing and successfully implemented regardless of race, religion or ethnicity. There is every indication of a real need for open discussion of how this concept could be implemented in the African American community in the Philadelphia area.

Feedback from the IESL Advisory Committee, comprised of professionals and community members representing a broad range of ethnic, racial and religious groups, indicates that interest is not limited to African Americans. As a result of displacement from Europe, Africa, Latin America and Asia, increasing numbers of individuals from other cultures are looking at the family reunion movement as the vehicle for enhancing family education and wealth creation.

MISSION

The mission of IESL is "Researching and Advocating Health, Education and Economic Literacy through Family Reunions". By positioning the family reunion movement as a vehicle, not only for teaching the language and concepts of how wealth is created, but also of implementing processes to obtain success in these areas, IESL has developed a paradigm shift for community development and empowerment. Another essential component of this empowerment is educating families on serious health issues that disproportion ally impact the African American community.

SHORT TERM GOALS

1. Gather a total of 1,500 Family Reunion Surveys in the Philadelphia area.

2. Using the Family Reunion Surveys, develop a Philadelphia area Family Reunion Registry. This will enable IESL, Inc. to reach out and garner support from the population to be served, as well as the African American religious institutions in the Philadelphia area.

3. Develop information and marketing materials to introduce the IESL mission and services to the initially targeted constituent group, African American families, as well as to the foundation and corporate communities.

4. Identify individuals, corporations and foundations that have an interest in fostering the health and economic literacy goals of IESL.

5. Using the Philadelphia Family Reunion Registry, contact African American families to obtain family medical histories.

6. Publish on a quarterly basis, a Family Reunion Newsletter, as a means of providing constituents with a description of how IESL implements its three program areas: Health, Education and Economic Literacy. The newsletter will also serve as the vehicle for educating African American families about the activities of the Family Reunion Movement across the country. Articles on how African American families have used their family reunions to empower themselves in the areas of wealth accumulation and sustainability as well as information on health issues impacting the African American community will be featured in each newsletter.

7. Raise awareness of the IESL mission and services on a city and state level via participation in multi-cultural forums.

8. With the assistance of the IESL Board and Advisory Committees, identify professionals capable of presenting topics such as: family medical histories, genetics and other health issues germane to African Americans; debt repair; credit development; asset accumulation and family educational Endowments/trusts.

9. Begin organizing for a September 2003 Family Reunion Expo to be held at a Temple University site by working with the Temple University Center for Public Policy. Identify hospitals; universities; corporations; tour/travel agencies; hotel/hospitality industry professionals; banking and investment firms; credit and debt repair, financial advisors and community vendors who would be interested in participation in this event.

10. Contract with an accredited agency to complete a program evaluation based on the following FY 2002/2003 activities:

    a. analysis of the data from the Family Reunion Registry

    b. review of the evaluation forms from Economic Literacy workshops presented to at least 6 African American churches in the Philadelphia Area

    c. distribution of the first IESL Family Reunion Newsletter

    d. progress on the November 2003 Family Reunion Expo

    It is the intent of IESL to use the city of Philadelphia as demonstration project from which a successful model can be developed and replicated in other major cities throughout the United States. Philadelphia will benefit directly from the coordination of family reunion activities, thereby increasing the tourist dollars being spent in the city.

LONG TERM GOALS

It is the intent of IESL to expand the family reunion from a purely social event into a vehicle for enhancement of family and individual health; education on the accumulation of assets; the maintenance of wealth and broader access to post secondary goals.

Health

Under the health component, individuals will have access to professionals who will provide healthy lifestyle, nutrition and preventive medicine information regarding major illnesses that impact the African American community. Family medical histories will be researched as a means of raising awareness of those who are at high risk of conditions such as high blood pressure, heart disease, sickle cell anemia and other genetically linked health problems and educate them on the means to avoid or ameliorate negative health outcomes.

Education and Economic Literacy

Under the wealth creation component, individuals will find a three-step process and will come in at whatever level they currently find themselves. The three levels will be it, debt repair/credit development; wealth accumulation and sustain ability and Lastly, family endowments/trusts and foundations, under which will be scholarships, micro enterprise/small business development activities, individual retirement accounts and family health insurance.

CHAPTER SIXTEEN
(RoughGemAuction.Com)

During my travels throughout several countries in Africa, notably South Africa, Angola, Botswana, Guinea and Sierra Leone, I began intimately familiar with the availability of rough gems and precious metals. I had numerous conversations with Ministers of Mines and Economic Development for these and other countries. One thing became increasingly clear to me, and that is that most of the countries are seeking an alternative means of bringing thee materials to the market.

As the result of a world wide monopoly on these items, the prices that are being paid are kept at a deflated by the cartels that exist to control the availability of these items. I am speaking primarily of diamonds, emeralds, Safire's and rubies, when it comes to precious stones, and Platinum, gold, silver when it comes to precious metals.

Several conversations center around the possibility of African American becoming involve in the trade of the items on a world wide basis. Concessions would be issued that would allow companies controlled by African Americans and in partnership with companies from the countries themselves that would allow, both the governments of these countries and the companies involved to reap vast profits from direct participation.

It has long been known that these are two of the surest methods of creating wealth, and have been for centuries. It is now time for the African American community to stake its claim on these natural resources in particular, and to use them to create companies that provide these items to the market within our communities.

There is no question but that African Americans spend an inordinate amount of money on jewelry, yet produce very little in the way of consumer ready products. This would change with the creation of RoughGemAuction. Com. An on line provider of rough gems and precious metals. Not only would RoughGemAuction be a supplier, but would set up businesses in our community to manufacture all manner of jewelry, which would be sold directly through churches and Mosques.

In conjunction with Ghenmor Import/Export Trading Co., Inc., RoughGemAuction.Com would form the basis for a full service provided of these products and services to the African American community. All aspects of the industry from farming rough stones in Africa to, cutting, polishing, cleaving, setting and mounting of stones in as per the requirements and design of our customers would be undertaken. Factory for the manufacture of jewelry would be set up in the community and experts would be trained in all aspects of this business.

Between 1996 and 1997 I attended the Gemological Institute of America, in Santa Monica, California and traveled extensively in Africa working and learning all aspects of the trade. There is not a group of individuals any where on the planet that loves jewelry as do we, and it only makes sense that we play a more prominent role in this industry.

This inter active web site will allow customers to not only chose the gem which they want, but also to determine what type of cut they would like the stone to be cut in. In addition the piece of jewelry can be designed, ordered and paid for online.

This will allow churches to play a very active role in the ownership and marketing of this business. From weddings to anniversaries, individuals will be able to through ownership in ESL to support a company in which they have a vested interest.

CHAPTER SEVENTEEN
(Family Corporation Workbook)

The philosophy and goal of IESL is to facilitate the development of corporate structures within the family unit. The highly celebrated and much anticipated occasion, known as the family reunion presents one of the most opportune moments in which a corporate entity can begin to be established. Utilizing a few moments at each reunion occasion to create an economic development forum, to discuss issues of financial security is perhaps the best investment of time and capital your family can make. With the assistance of this IESL workbook and CD Rom study guide each family will learn how to ensure the stability of your family's economic future.

Once the formation of your family corporation is completed, each family member can access the benefits of debt protections and fiscal; opportunities that corporate empires have enjoyed for years. Issues such as: debt repair, credit development, asset accumulation, capital formation, educational endowments, mutual funds, home ownership, prepaid financial services. These are just a few benefits the entire family will be able to enjoy.

IESL has developed a CD-ROM, as a study guide designed to assist your family's delegated family members, who will be filing the necessary forms to establish your own corporate empire. The CD's main purpose is to accompany the IESL Family Corporation Workbook.

It is through the active administration and collection of nearly six thousand family reunion use surveys that have enable IESL to develop a perfect vehicle that can transport our community from impoverishment to empowerment. ESL is a dynamic do-it-yourself program specifically designed to build wealth. As previously indicated, family reunions offer the perfect starting point for transforming the unlimited financial potential that is inherent in all family units, into an organized structure known as a family corporation.

The sequence, in which the contents of the workbook are introduced, is the order in which the documents should be prepared. At the end of the process, a recommended systematic approach is outlined for submission of the documents to attain maximum effective and efficient results.

Chapter I – By Laws

Article I – deals with the name and purpose of the organization.

Article II – deals with the membership of the Board of Directors, for the corporation. Directors are elected by the members of the family at the annual meeting (reunion) of the family unit. Membership should be limited to the Board of Directors of the corporation for voting purposes of the corporation. Advisory plebiscites should be held on major questions confronting the family corporation.

Article III – deals with the annual meeting, which will be held at the family reunion each year.

Article IV – deals with the Board of Directors, its meetings, which will be held at the family reunion each year.

Chapter II – Articles of incorporation

Articles of Incorporation vary from State to State and address the critical areas of incorporation. Firstly, the not for profit corporation law of the State in which you will be incorporated, depends upon where the family considers its original place of origin. The corporation could be incorporated in that State.

The draft copy of articles in the workbook represents a style of articles of incorporations, which have been widely accepted as representative of what, the government requires.

Chapter III – Form SS4, Application for Employer Identification Number

This form is used to establish a corporation, under the department of the treasury of the Internal Revenue Service. This will allow the corporation to acquire and employee identification number. The following lines must be filled out accordingly:

1. The legal name of the corporation

2. N/A

3. Individual doing incorporation

4a. Mailing address for the business

4b. City, State and Zip code

5a. N/A

5b. N/A

6. County where corporation is located

7a. Name of principle officer

7b. N/A

8a. The type of entity is (other) non profit

8b. N/A

9. Started new business

10. Date business started

11. June

12. N/A

13. Agriculture 0   Household 0   Other 0

14. Other (specify) family corporation

15. None

16a.No

16b.N/A

For further instructions, call 1-866-816-2065, and speak with a representative of the Internal Revenue Service to acquire and EIN, which follows you as your family corporation grows and flourishes.

Chapter IV – Form 1023 Application for Recognition of Exemption, Under Section 501 ©3 of the Internal Revenue Code

Part I   Identification of Applicant

PartII   Activities and Operational Information

PartIII   Technical requirements

PartIV   Financial Data

Chapter V – Form 8718 User Fee for Exempt Organization Determination Letter Request

The type of request for your corporation will make is, 3aa, with a deposit of $150.00 by check, money order or bank check.

Chapter VI – Form 872C, Consent Fixing Period of Limitation upon Assessment of Tax under Section 4940 of the Internal Revenue Code

Ending date of first tax year is June 30th of the current year, if it is before June that you are filling out forms, or of the following year, if after June 30th of the current year.

Chapter VII – Miscellaneous

Also enclosed is a draft copy of an executive summary, budget, a budget narrative, and a work plan. These sample copies will assist the family corporation in drawing up its own documents that reflect your family's goals and objectives.

Chapter VIII – Order of Submission

Following this order is critical to the short-term and long-term success of the corporation. The first order of business is as follows:

1. Completion of the SS4 form. At this point call the number supplied with the form. Give this information to the Internal Revenue Service, at which time they will supply you with an EIN. This number will then be listed on all subsequent submissions, when called for.

2. Put together Articles of Incorporation and By-Laws for the corporation.

3. Complete form 1023.

4. Submit Articles of Incorporation to the State Bureau of Corporations for the State in which you desire to be incorporated.

5. Once the Articles are sealed or certified by the State Bureau of Corporations they will be returned to you, at which time you will forward them, along with the form 1023 application, a copy of your by-laws, a copy of the 8718 form, two (2) copies of form 872-C, to the Internal Revenue Service at 201 West Rivercenter Blvd. Attn: Extracting Stop 312, Covington, Kentucky 41011 as listed on form 8718.

Chapter IX – Budgets, work plans and executive summaries

While waiting for the return of these important documents, which generally take 120 days, it is advisable to begin to lay the groundwork for the work of your family corporation. In other words, what businesses will your family corporation be involved in? And where and how will it function?

Chapter X – Form 990 – Schedule A

Tax form required only after Family Corporation has employees.

Chapter XI – Joining the Institute for Economics as a Second Language, Inc.

In order to become a member of IESL, it will be necessary for you to fill out the application form, which you will find in the addendums. The fees are arranged according to the level of membership that you want. Bronze at $250.00. Silver at $500.00 and Gold at $900.00. This provides your family corporation with a life time membership in the Institute for Economics as a Second Language, Inc.

IESL's goal is to organize ten thousand family corporations into a mass movement to transform the dissemination of wealth related information and opportunities which will allow for the formation of a base for wealth in our community unlike any that has ever existed before.

IESL will provide for the collective economic empowerment to make possible the construction and operation of international resorts, for families to hold their reunions all over the world. Please become a member of IESL and help your family, along with families from around the country to reach their full financial potential.

We recommend whole-heartedly that you seize this moment and learn how to better protect and serve your family's financial interest. Join us in this national network for wealth creation call the Family Reunion Economic empowerment movement.

PRAYER OF JABEZ

And Jabez called on the God of Israel saying, "Oh, that you would bless me indeed, and enlarge my territory, that your hand would be with me, and that you would keep me from evil, that I may not cause pain." So God granted him what he requested.